Visible

OTHER TITLES IN THE
CALICO SERIES

That We May Live:
Speculative Chinese Fiction

Home: Arabic Poems

Elemental: Earth Stories

Cuíer: Queer Brazil

This Is Us Losing Count:
Eight Russian Poets

Visible

Text + Image

CALICO

"Un pas de chat sauvage" by Marie NDiaye © Flammarion, Paris, 2019. Photograph by Nadar (Gaspard-Félix Tournachon) printed alongside story with permission from the Bibliothèque Nationale de France © Musées d'Orsay et de l'Orangerie, Paris, 2019.

Emily Yae Won's translation of "As boats and buses go by" by Yi SangWoo originally published in *Busan Biennale 2020 Words at an Exhibition* 열 장의 이야기와 다섯 편의 시 [*an exhibition in ten chapters and five poems*]. Curated by Jacob Fabricius.

Excerpt from Piotr Paziński's *The Boarding House* published here in Scotia Gilroy's translation with permission from Dalkey Archive; *The Boarding House* was published in 2018 in MJ Dabrowska's translation.

Quatrain from 證道歌 by Yongjia Xuanjue translated from Chinese by Lucas Klein and published with his permission.

Additional credits appear on pages 213–214.

Visible is sixth in the Calico Series.

Two Lines Press
582 Market Street, Suite 700, San Francisco, CA 94104
www.twolinespress.com

ISBN: 978-1-949641-37-0

Cover design by Crisis
Cover image © Rodrigo Flores Sánchez, created in conjunction with Paulina Barraza G.
Typesetting and interior design by LOKI
Printed in the United States of America

Library of Congress Cataloging-in-Publication Data

TITLE: Visible: text + image.
DESCRIPTION: San Francisco, CA : Two Lines Press, [2022] | Series: Calico series; 6 | English translations of French, Korean, Polish, and Spanish works. | Summary: "Six genre-defying works that blend text and images. Includes illustrations, memes, and photographs alongside poems, reportage, and fiction" -- Provided by publisher.
IDENTIFIERS: LCCN 2022001499 | ISBN 9781949641370 (paperback)
SUBJECTS: LCSH: Fiction--Translations into English. | Poetry, Modern--20th century--Translations into English. | Poetry, Modern--21st century--Translations into English. | LCGFT: Fiction. | Poetry.
CLASSIFICATION: LCC PN6120.2 .V57 2022 | DDC 808.8/0110905--dc23/eng/20220216
LC record available at https://lccn.loc.gov/2022001499

THIS BOOK WAS PUBLISHED WITH SUPPORT FROM THE NATIONAL ENDOWMENT FOR THE ARTS.

NATIONAL ENDOWMENT for the ARTS
arts.gov

Words

and Images

Verónica Gerber Bicecci

Translated from Spanish by Christina MacSweeney

WORDS AND IMAGES*

Verónica Gerber Bicecci

Translated by
Christina MacSweeney

*A re-writing of "Les mots et les images" by René Magritte, "La Révolution surréaliste", 1929.

An image and a word can be equivalent:

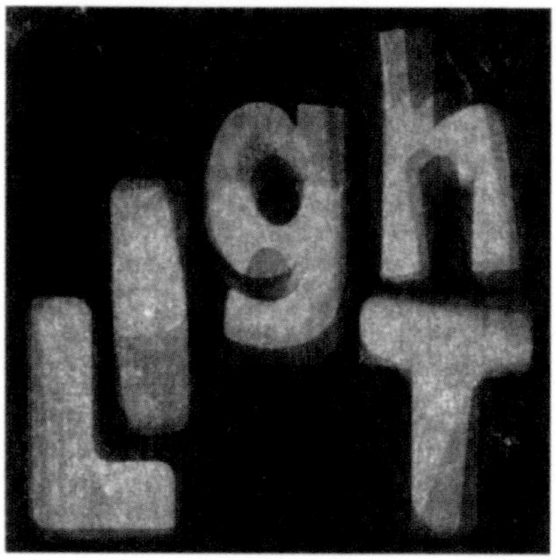
LighT

(sun print)

Some words are incapable of forming an image:

future

Some images don't completely match the words they refer to:

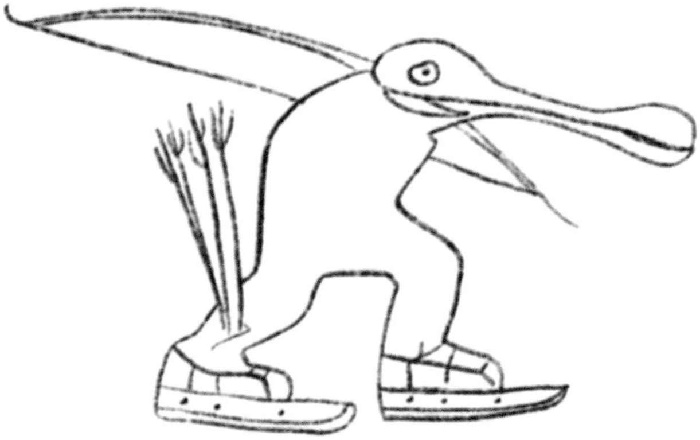

(Hieronimus Bosch, "The Garden of Earthly Delights
1490-1510, detail)

An image can explain a text;
that is called illustration:

OPTICAL ILLUSION

(Anon)

A text can explain an image;
that is called iconization:

DANGER

(Anon)

The image-text relationship
is inescapable. In fact, there
is no difference between them,
only a problem known as
logocentrism:

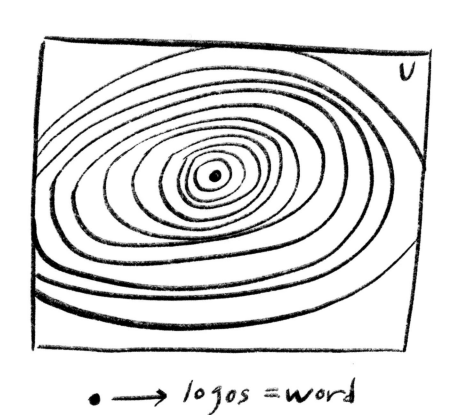

• ——→ logos = word

Logocentrism tends to make us
believe that images don't think:

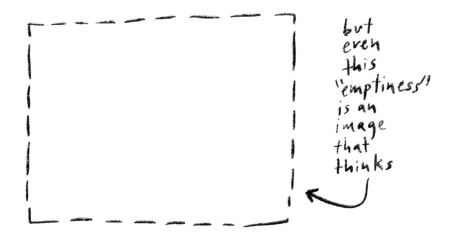

but
even
this
"emptiness"
is an
image
that
thinks

When images and words
come together it is
called a diagram. In
this case they are
complementary:

W   I

Every W is an I

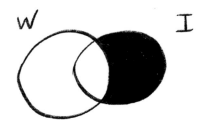

W   I

Every I is a W

W: word
I: image

A diagram can suggest that
there are other spaces besides
equivalence, illustration, iconization
and complementarity for thinking
about the relationships between
images and words:

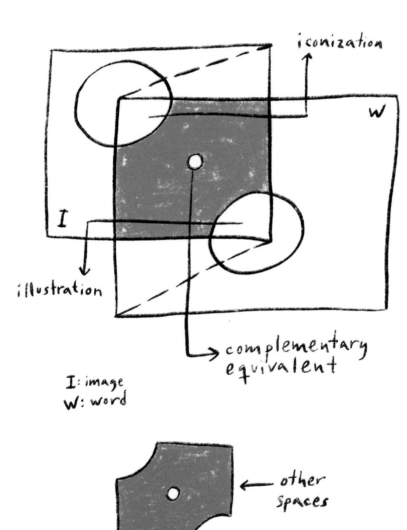

iconization

W

I

illustration

complementary
equivalent

I: image
W: word

other
spaces

Words and images are a single language that is read in (at least) two different ways:

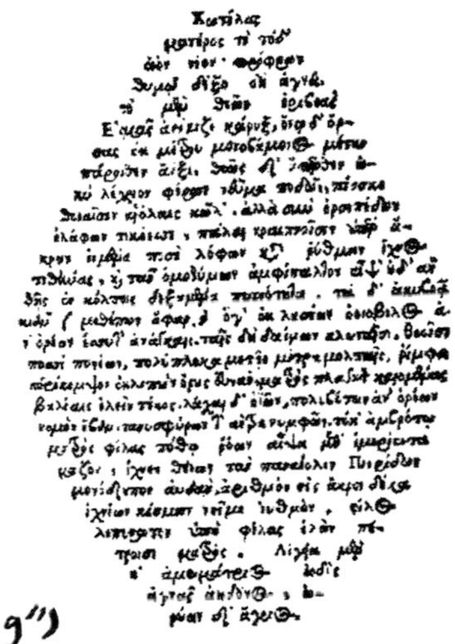

(Simmias of Rhodes, c. 4th century BC, "Egg")

The image and text of a calligram can never be read at the same time:

egg (n). 1a: the hard-shelled reproductive body produced by a bird and especially by the common domestic chicken *also*: its contents used as food; 1b: an animal reproductive body consisting of an ovum together with its nutritive and protective envelopes and having the capacity to develop into a new individual capable of independent existence; 1c: OVUM.
2: something resembling an egg.
3: Sort of person (a good egg); have egg on one's face: a state of embarrassment or humiliation.

(from Webster and RAE dictionaries)

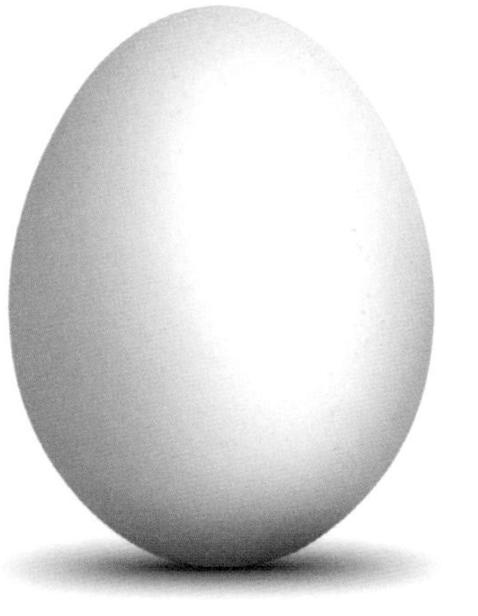

(Anon)

Reading an image involves
encoding its ideas into words:

Reading a text involves
decoding its ideas
into images:

The internet is the most complex calligram in existence: a network of image-text connections in an "invisible" space, ruled by algorithms and with an interface of users:

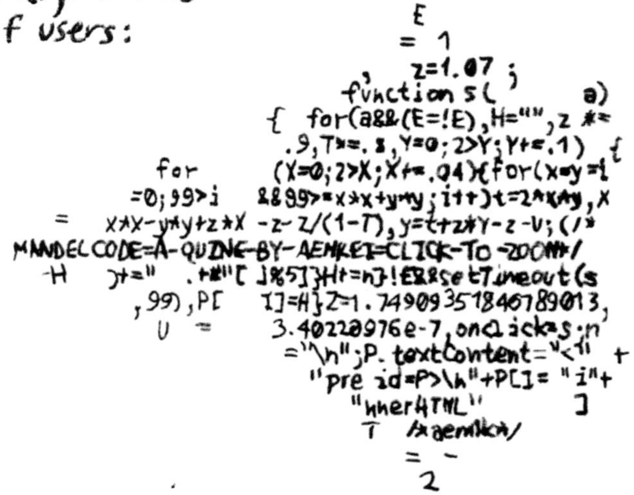
E
= 1
z=1.07 ;
function s(a)
{ for(a&&(E=!E),H="",z *=
.9,T*=.8,Y=0;2>Y;Y+=.1) {
for (X=0;2>X;X+=.04){for(x=y=i
=0;99>i &&99>=x*x+y*y;i++)t=2*x*y,x
= x*x-y*y+z*X -z-Z/(1-T),y=t+z*Y-z-V;(/*
MANDELCODE=A-QUINE-BY-AEMKEI=CLICK-TO-ZOOM*/
H)+=" .+*"[i%5]}H+=n}!E&&setTimeout(s
,99),P[I]=H}Z=1.74909351840789013,
V = 3.40220976e-7,onclick=s;n
="\n";P.textContent="<" +
"pre id=P>\n"+P[I]= "i"+
"nnerHTML"]
T /*aemkei*/
= -
2
(from code-poetry com)

So, emojis now also have important, essential meanings within our messages. The image-text adds a new dimension to our modes of communication:

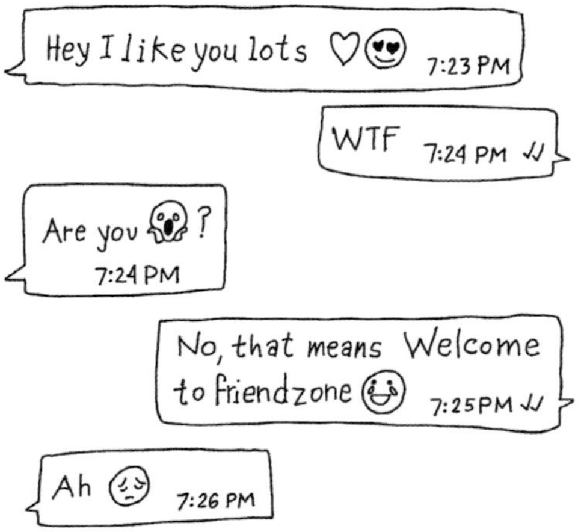
Hey I like you lots ♡😍 7:23 PM
WTF 7:24 PM
Are you 😱? 7:24 PM
No, that means Welcome to friendzone 😉 7:25 PM
Ah 😔 7:26 PM

(Anon)

Memes, for example, are calligrams.

They
sometimes
encode
intangible
problems:

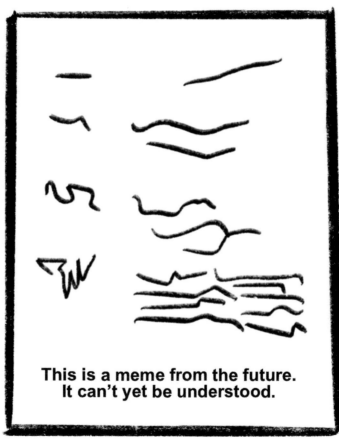

**This is a meme from the future.
It can't yet be understood.**

(Anon)

They
sometimes
encode
concrete
problems:

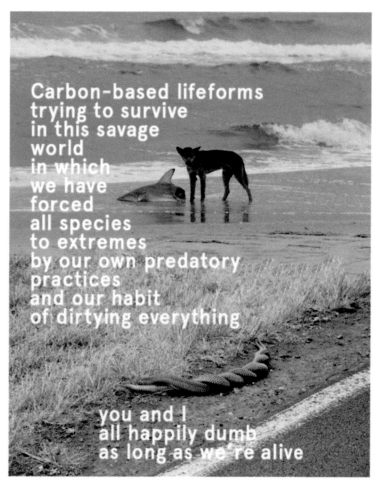

Carbon-based lifeforms
trying to survive
in this savage
world
in which
we have
forced
all species
to extremes
by our own predatory
practices
and our habit
of dirtying everything

you and I
all happily dumb
as long as we're alive

(by brokeneglish.lol, 2018)

We don't live in the age of
the image:

CALLIGR IN THE · AGE WE LIVE GRAMATICA

Step

of a

Feral

Cat

Marie NDiaye

Translated from French by Victoria Baena

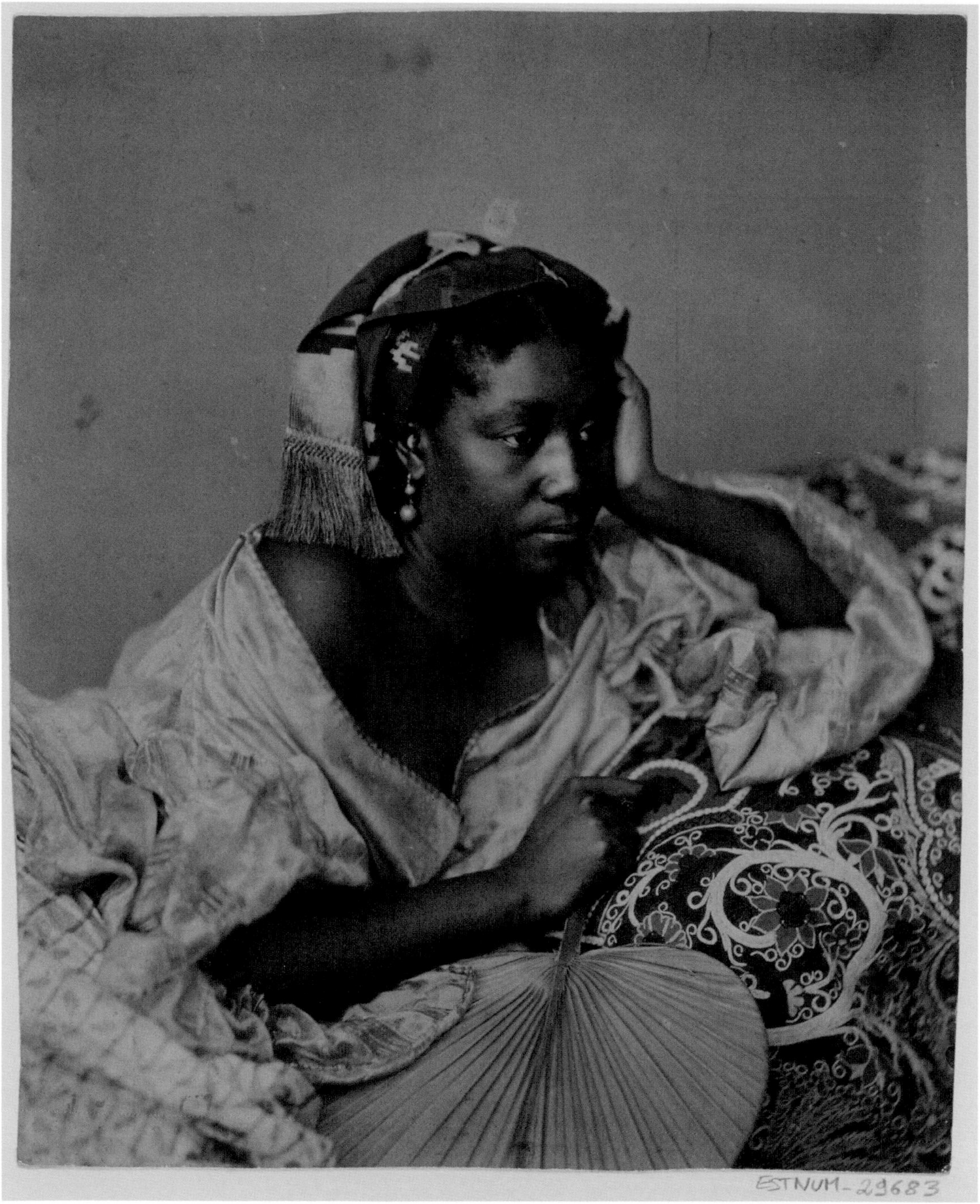
ESTNUM-29683

In 2008, I received my first email from a certain Marie Sachs (the name is invented, it feels more prudent not to reveal her last name, less to protect her from any unflattering comments or judgments—which she by no means deserves!—but rather, if she does ever manage to bring her big idea to fruition, to avoid casting a shadow over her work of the missteps that prevented it from taking shape earlier, in which case one would view the finished product from a different perspective, registering only the obstacles overcome, the labor and the effort), from a certain Marie Sachs asking to meet with me so that I could share with her some of my research on Maria Martinez.

Something unpleasant, insistent, and imperious in the tone of this message, something strangely panting too (as if each word were breathless), dissuaded me from responding.

I even marked the sender as spam without further thought.

And yet, thus reassured that I would never again see Marie Sachs's name in my inbox, I caught myself repeating the exact words of her request. I realized I had unintentionally memorized her query, and that I must have spent some nights unconsciously asking the search engine to tell me everything it knew about Marie Sachs.

For even if I remembered nothing about the search itself, I did recall precisely what it had shown me.

At night, I only surf the web drunk.

That's why I sometimes wholly forget that I've done so, that I've spent hours at the computer attempting to penetrate certain mysteries, to grasp all at once what had previously been hidden from me, knowledge without which, I then feel, I could not fall sleep, I could never fall asleep again.

When I awaken, I remember nothing of those disturbing hours, those deeply intellectual, haunted hours.

But I do, prodigiously, remember each line I read, as one occasionally remembers the smallest, most precise detail of a dream even when no longer recalling the room or the bed where it took shape.

So it was that, on December 25, 2008, as I lifted my glass for a Christmas toast, I vowed never to meet Marie Sachs, and yet, at exactly that same moment, just as two photographic negatives overlap and the features of one mix inextricably with the other, my mind retraced Marie Sachs's various works, perhaps I should call them experiments or delusions, though the web had only been able to give me a rough outline of them, even after long, muddled hours of navigation.

"How is your research on Maria Martinez going?" my nephew asked me good-naturedly as we were finishing a lavish lunch that Christmas day in 2008.

He added, with the gentle intention of showing me that he did in fact remember what I had told him, "The Black Malibran?"

Dismayed to realize that I must have spoken about my subject,

30

perhaps a long time ago already, though I didn't remember doing so, and that I had been so unthinking, so undiscerning, in going against my usual rules of secrecy, I quickly responded that I was getting nowhere, that I wasn't finding much, that I was probably even going to give up.

And at the same time the certainty of the exact opposite caused a painful throbbing between my brows—I would never abandon my project of writing a great, long novel on the life of Maria Martinez.

I asked my nephew, "Are you in touch with Marie Sachs?"

"Marie who?"

"How could a stranger know about my research? I talked to you about it, it seems. Was there anyone else?"

"How could I know?"

His little laugh was affectionately complicit.

Still, as I took out my loose tobacco, he pinched his thin lips and shook his head with such hostility that childish tears came to my eyes, sudden, acidic, and quickly suppressed.

Over the course of the following year, 2009, my confidence in my own abilities, my conviction that with enough tenacity I would accomplish my goals, collided with the patent fact that I knew far too little about Maria Martinez to be able to imagine anything at all about her.

I knew nothing of her childhood, nor of that kind of childhood in general, in Havana at the beginning of the nineteenth century, and how could I, how dare I invent what I didn't know anything about, this was hampering the historian and the university professor in me.

In my despondency, and as I was looking over the scant biographical coordinates that I had collected on the topic of Maria Martinez for the thousandth time, it occurred to me, not without bitterness, that

Marie Sachs would not trouble herself over such scruples and would undoubtedly make Maria Martinez into a character of her own invention, which she would exploit for her own artistic ends, not to do her justice, as I myself aspired to.

I knew, of course, that her memory could be vindicated if I simply exposed her own insolent genius, offering to the world the forgotten, enigmatic, and poignant profile of a talented and martyred woman, all while revealing the audacity, the perspicacity, the luminous vision of the author herself through the splendor of her narrative as well as by the very fact that she had chosen such a subject.

I knew all that and I did think that Marie Sachs ought to work that way, sacrificing herself sincerely, gloriously, in order to express the way in which another woman, in another time, had been sacrificed (without glory, without her consent).

I came to feel a strange jealousy toward Marie Sachs, attributing to her a presumptuousness and an arrogance that I lacked.

And how had she learned that I was working on Maria Martinez?

What did she know about her, what did she want to do with her?

Was it not my duty to protect Maria Martinez from the falsified portraits that a young, extravagant, ambitious artist might wish to fashion out of the little that we know of her, all the more so without being sure it's really her?

For there is Maria Martinez the dancer and musician, and there is Maria the *Antillaise* photographed by Nadar, and even if I am firmly convinced that these two Marias are the same person, it is impossible for me to prove it.

I could not allow myself, I then reasoned, not to mention in my own book this doubt, this suspicion, this demoralizing possibility that the face captured by Nadar, which had instilled in me such a desire for narrative and for romance, might have no link with that Martinez of whom I did know something, not much but still enough to start me thinking that I had to write her story.

Marie Sachs, I said to myself, would not hesitate to take for granted that the woman in the photographs was indeed Maria Martinez, she would not try to prove anything but would assert her will and ardor to the point of obliterating any demand for truth.

Since I could not remember when and with whom I had spoken about Maria Martinez, and since I could not figure out why Marie Sachs had decided to contact me, I plunged again into one of those haggard, hallucinatory nights, disconcerting after the fact but necessary to my ability to enjoy life, in the course of which I descend into the abyss of the internet until that point when everything suddenly becomes clear, when I realize that there's never any mystery, any ambiguity to be found, when existence itself becomes simple and right, never shameful.

This time I went in search of my own name, my own words—any decisive and absentminded words that might have escaped me during some inconsequential interview, only to be overlaid with thousands, millions of other words until my own disappeared into the depths of that global network.

Nevertheless, I found nothing, in any language (I speak several)—not an interview, not a mere moment from a conference, not a tweet, in fact it seemed that on this subject my memory had not deceived me and that no one in the world, apart from my nephew, could have known that Maria Martinez was currently my main point of interest.

Who, then, was Marie Sachs to me?

Did she know that I had not yet written a single line, was she somehow looking over my shoulder, was her mind lodged within mine?

Did she guess that I had hung the two portraits of Maria Martinez opposite my desk and that, in scrutinizing them before setting to work in vain, I would get lost in moral scruples that prevented me from looking at her face, its dry perspicacity being just what I needed, I told myself, in order to write about her?

I felt that if I paid close enough attention I might discern the subtle principle animating Maria Martinez, and sometimes I could even feel her gentle breath on my forehead, over my eyes, and I would blink and silently whisper tangled excuses to this woman, whose life, I hoped, would reinvigorate my own.

I would, I thought, have to unmask Maria Martinez's aura, which I discerned so intensely in the portraits, for the benefit of my work—as unknown, obscure (and indeed only imagined, never achieved) as it might be—and at the expense of this departed soul's right not to be turned over to the passion of just anyone.

Yet I did have hesitations, mystical fears as well as a feminine reticence (what truth about contemporary female life could I hope to grind out of the life of another woman?) that, I believed, prevented me alone from troubling her repose.

That spring of 2009, I didn't yet dare admit that I simply did not know how to do it, how to leave behind the troubled reveries into which the gaze of the photographed Maria Martinez would throw me—a haughty gaze, or at least one careful to seem so at the moment the shots had been taken, to activate such reveries, their consequences and their impact—and how to express them, whether in the voice of Maria Martinez, which never came to me, not even in a dream; in my own, which often caused me great shame; or in another voice altogether, one which might unite our two vulnerable minds with its own: purer, more impressive, more hospitable.

It was in this state of great psychological fragility, and once I had added my daily dose of a dash of cocaine to the gin and tonics that served as my meals, that I wrote to Marie Sachs, with impulsiveness, desperation, brutality, as if I were laying siege to a deserted, ruined palace—not Marie Sachs's soul but, in truth, my own.

Something of this cesspool persisted, wanting obdurately to live, while my evil genie did its utmost to pillage it, and even if I felt at times, overcome by rancor beyond belief, that Marie Sachs was somehow the guilty party, in some way I could not quite define, I also felt that she alone (unveiling her face, discerning who she was) would allow me to once again find a way of inhabiting the place from which I had banished myself.

I saw in Maria Martinez integrity, vehement obstinacy, bravery, and pride, all qualities that I had long ago surrendered.

Who was Maria Martinez, model of Nadar?

I didn't know.

But she was inevitably more valiant, tougher, braver than me in every way, and spending time with her, if I ever managed to draw closer, would draw me out of myself, I thought, out of my misery, my foolishness, my bitter womanly void, sardonic and cold and sleeping too little, dreaming too rarely of scenes simple and benign.

Marie Sachs responded at once.

Rather, she explained, than setting a meeting in a café, which risked a kind of awkwardness, possibly irreparable, slipping between us, given the obligation to speak cheerfully and with good humor even though we didn't know and couldn't be sure that we would like each other, she invited me to hear her perform at the Alhambra, where she would be singing and dancing, so that she could give me a sense of herself and her character without the discomfort of meeting one-on-one, and she concluded, strangely, "You'll have to see if Maria Martinez continues to keep you company."

She also informed me, in a pleasant tone and yet taking care not to rob her words of their gravity, that I should respond in kind to anything she gave me, at least depending on how much I liked the show, and not hide from her anything that I had learned about Maria Martinez—actually she didn't quite master syntax or grammar, she wrote that she wanted to know what I had learned "on" Maria Martinez, which I internally corrected to "about."

I know now that she had written precisely what she had meant.

I was, at that time, too haughty and too addicted to my own intelligence to understand this.

I thought about Marie Sachs, my eyes half-shut. My interest in her was impassioned but covetous, selfish. We had nothing in common; she was an obscure woman.

From what I could tell, she was not a highly educated woman.

Besides, she was an artist that no one important had written about, whether to praise or to pan her—the only remarks I had unearthed consisted of interjections that I did not know how to interpret, that alarmed and disoriented me, preventing me from continuing; I didn't like finding myself in bad company, not even on the web.

So it was that on a November evening, as a thick rain was falling, I left my home on Boulevard Rochechouart for the first time in days, with nothing covering my head.

I had misplaced my umbrella, if I had ever had one.

But comfort and ease barely mattered to me.

In the hall of the Alhambra, I sat down right in front, the little round table was sticky, my face was washed, my hair dripping, I felt uncertain.

I had so little patience for cabarets, for music halls!

The room quickly filled and, sensing the presence of so many people behind me, whose interest in Marie Sachs I found incomprehensible, I regretted not having chosen a seat in the back, sheltered from their ecstatic breathing.

Everything here felt foreign, hostile even, to me.

Even Maria Martinez's face, which never left my mind, became foggy, as if I suddenly needed her less, as if she might be in the way, might prevent me from stepping cheerfully toward a clean and proper future.

It did not fall silent when Marie Sachs stepped on stage: to the contrary.

I knew nothing about how things worked here.

Yet I had the impression that the mundane murmur of conversations had subtly altered and that there was some scandalized and mocking reaction rising at my back, disgruntled and heated, as if, I immediately thought, even though the spectators had expected what they were now facing, they were nonetheless angry, aggravated, if not surprised.

Marie Sachs had appeared all at once, as if she had emerged not from the wings but from the faintly smoky atmosphere, suddenly there she was, motionless.

A very soft tone rose from her barely unsealed lips, a song made up of words I could not understand in a language I could not identify.

She strummed the strings of a small guitar.

Her shoulders, chest, waistline were bared.

She had a dark complexion, her skin shone like high-grade leather.

Her breasts were of medium size, pert and high.

She was wearing a long and ample floral-print skirt, its volume probably amplified by other skirts beneath it, and green, a dark, murky green, seemed to be the dominant tone for that skirt that descended to just above Marie Sachs's feet.

I was so disconcerted that I had to shut my eyes for a long moment.

But with my eyes closed it was even more difficult to bear the bizarre, untimely, incongruous song of Marie Sachs.

I could not judge it in terms of approval, nor in terms of pleasure or displeasure.

I did not understand what this voice, this chant, was unleashing within me nor the emotion forcing me to close my eyes and then open them again with no more clarity as to whether my panicked heart was the better for it. My gaze wandered from the stage to the audience, from the curtains to the ground, where it remained, mute, stupefied, yet unquiet.

I heard exclamations burst forth, stunned and mocking without undermining Marie Sachs's performance whatsoever, and it seemed that no one was leaving, no one laughing contemptuously, even if I thought I heard fierce snickers, and the turbulence fizzled out on its own while the voice of Marie Sachs—which the sour notes of the guitar seemed less to accompany than to strain to reproduce—her keen and ethereal voice, bitter, precise, and difficult, triumphed over the audience's aversion, even as the latter, evidently, was hardly seduced.

I felt as though that body, that skin, bared in all simplicity, that proud and cold gaze, that chant arising out of nowhere were getting the better of us, and that our perplexity and aversion could not last long against Marie Sachs's proud obstinacy, against her stubborn, dauntless, boundless resistance.

We felt flustered and futile, easily provoked.

She was tenacious, stoic, and the hours belonged to her, she was bare and impenetrable, strange and tranquil, we could not upset her so easily, in her serene zealotry.

Despite knowing quite well that our email exchanges had tacitly implied I would wait for her at the exit of the Alhambra or would meet her at her dressing room, I went home as soon as the show was over, too filled with emotion to consider meeting Marie Sachs in the heat of the moment and feeling incapable of commenting on what I had heard—congratulating her, but in what sense, on which aspects of the performance?

As far as critique, I do that frequently and without any particular discomfiture, even face-to-face with the person subjected to my inexorably correct opinion—but what severe or disappointed statement could I make on Marie Sachs's undefinable voice, on the act in its entirety, which I could not connect to anything I knew, which I could not even critically compare with the work of any other artist?

I received a text message from Marie Sachs as soon as I arrived home.

She asked me, in a light tone, if Maria Martinez had reaped positive reviews after her first singing tour in Paris, in the Salle Herz, and what her feelings then had been.

I responded immediately, without bothering to take off my coat, my wet shoes, that the reviews had been condescending, mocking, though rather mild if you accept the idea that goodwill can be mixed with disdain and disrespect, that the will to protect and to champion can rest on insult and offense.

Negroes have their own music, *Bamboula*, national tunes, which they repeat day and night to their hearts' content, but never abandon, and which help them to cheerfully overcome their workdays, to enliven their extravagant dances, to fall asleep after the sun's rays fade, in sweet nightly dreams. It is thus something new for a Negress musician, educated in the fundamentals of song, to sing with intelligence and to render hints of love, sadness, and joy with her voice.
—*Le Nouvelliste*, June 13, 1850

We have finally heard that famous Black Malibran, and our lyrical pens have duly attempted to give a first-class rendering.

Doña Maria Martinez has just given a concert in the Salle Herz. Alas! We are obligated to lower the volume for all the preemptive publicity poured over that Negro throat. Either Doña Maria Martinez only ever had a bad voice and a method to match, or else the Parisian climate, we must accept, has greatly spoiled this exotic product.
—*Le Ménestrel*, June 16, 1850

The success of this Negress was real: she tastefully delivered some Spanish tunes, accompanying herself on the guitar, and drawing applause from the audience. Madame Maria Martinez is of medium height and fine appearance; the color of her skin is almost black at her face, but lightens at the neck and shoulders, leading one to assume that she is a motley-complexioned Negress; though this is not so.
—*Le Tintamarre*, June 23, 1850

In terms of Maria Martinez's feelings, I confessed to Marie Sachs that I did not dare, was too reticent, to picture them.

I added all the same that ordeals, heartbreak, and sorrow had suffused her life from childhood, that Maria Martinez could only be considered strong, tenacious, and remarkable in managing to get herself to Paris from Havana where she had been born, and that, thanks to such mental force, the jeers had not profoundly affected her, while the compliments and marks of affection had played an enlivening role, I would think.

For otherwise, how could she have endured?

I went on, explaining to Marie Sachs that I felt an unfailing gratitude toward Théophile Gautier, who had generously worked to make a name for Maria Martinez.

He had, I felt, been kind to her, though here too it should be granted that at times something mean or underhanded can find its way into kindness (doesn't he refer to her in one letter—ironically, to be sure—as a monkey?), at the very least it should be granted that courtesy, intelligence, tact might all give way to the doubtful pleasure of such a choice word.

But, I continued, without Théophile Gautier, Maria Martinez would not have sung and played like she did in her first years in Paris, that's why, I thought, you could not, if you carried Maria within yourself, feel anything other than honest gratitude toward Théophile Gautier.

He was her friend, so quite simply I made him mine.

I was still in the entranceway to my apartment, still wearing my coat.

Every day, when I wake up, I wrote to Marie Sachs, the first image in my head is of Maria Martinez.

I closed my telephone, abruptly worn out from talking to Marie Sachs in that way.

But she sent me another message:

What about me, what do you think I felt tonight?

I responded, vaguely annoyed, that I did not have the least idea.

At the instant when, having sent the message, I realized it was untrue, she was already responding that all the same I had to try to approach the question, no matter my professorial reticence (she concluded mockingly).

I felt dumb, not up to the task, I was ashamed I had felt it necessary to show my arrogant side.

So, when she invited me to come listen to her again, at a different address, I quickly accepted.

This time it was an apartment on the Boulevard Saint-Germain, at the home of a certain couple, the Bastiers.

Marie Sachs had let them know I was coming, she gave me the three codes I would need to reach their door, on the second floor of a swollen building, bursting with stucco, caryatids, columns.

A housekeeper with very dark skin showed me into a living room already filled with visitors, and when this housekeeper left, Marie Sachs, seated on a low platform, remained the only black woman and the only young woman in the group, which I noticed with an uneasy feeling of sadness, for, since Maria Martinez had entered my life, I had vehemently and grimly aspired to become a young black woman.

But the small blunt voice that always entered my dreams to contradict the few images of bliss assured me that this would never happen, that this indulgent and absurd desire could never be granted, that I would never again be young and happy and free and that to the contrary I was ever more rapidly taking on the kinds of traits, silhouettes, complexions that I saw in the Bastier couple to whom the housekeeper had introduced me, two elderly people with similar faces, fixed in contrition and a kind of permanent alarm.

This expression of solemnity did not change when Marie Sachs launched into her strange songs.

Perhaps she even intensified, all too slightly, the anxiety that gave the couple's seriousness a funereal aura (as if they feared death crouching behind a chair and pouncing on them).

Their guests, in fact, at first maintained an attitude toward Marie Sachs that I found irreverent before realizing that it was certainly the only possible attitude, the only one that Marie Sachs herself could have desired and to which she did not attribute any malicious intent (how could they have wanted to appear unobliging to their hosts, who were introducing Marie Sachs, offering her to them?) but only an extraordinary urge to abandon their insincere, fastidious, and morbid manners.

So it was that these well-heeled elderly people began to whistle jeeringly, snickering indiscreetly, clearing their throats ostentatiously to signify that something, to their mind, was not right, all this under the tormented gaze of the Bastier couple who nonetheless retained great fortitude, for, if their eyes flew back and forth like madmen, not a word of explanation or justification or even excuse or regret ever crossed their lips.

And when, after thirty minutes, Marie Sachs's song was grasped and acknowledged in its eccentricity, when her guitar went silent, no longer struck in that way so as to imitate her astounding voice, and there descended over the room a certain calm, though with the faded taunts still reverberating, the Bastiers slackened imperceptibly, their feverish expressions ceased fluttering and finally came to rest on the object of their veneration, smoldering serenely, as close as possible to Marie Sachs.

She was wearing a long, straight dress, pale gray and glittery, and it seemed to me that things were also sparkling in her upswept hair, on her forehead, at her ears.

She was elegant and refined in an unusual way, which forced you to observe her, to reflect, then to decide if it was actually elegance, actually refinement.

It seemed obvious then that it was—yet this was deceiving, it had not been obvious but quite uncertain, contestable in the intimacy of each person's contemplation.

Marie Sachs's breasts, which I had seen free and exposed at the Alhambra, were compressed, almost crushed by the very tight bodice of her dress.

She no longer had much cleavage in this outfit, and so I had to assume that she must have painfully bandaged her torso to get this result, and for what?

I knew the words to the last song that she performed, written by Théophile Gautier for Maria Martinez, so well that I murmured in unison with her:

If I am black, I am a woman
The French audience is gallant
I have hopes for it, I profess it
More than my own modest talent
From your France to art so precious
Messieurs, *sustain today*

Your renowned hospitality
Welcome this poor foreign woman

Marie Sachs had taken on the voice of a dying little girl for this song, so deliberately pathetic as to be comical.

Yet no one smiled or raised their eyebrows, either ironically or discomfited, and I thought then that Marie Sachs had achieved the feat of shutting the door to all possible derision, after having, in a way, invited it, spurred it on, from the start of her show.

"If I am black, I am a woman": she was perfectly capable of singing this, I recognized now, with modesty and tact.

She had chosen the indecency of melodrama, she was regal, sarcastic, likewise harsh, vengeful, and bitter.

They eat out of my dark, cold little hand, in everything I act as I wish and according to my own design, there's no manner of scorn that can touch me.

She was met with extended applause, even though the Bastiers, who had gone up to the platform next to her and were framing her with their two fixed silhouettes, kept a perpetually watchful lookout, as if searching the shadowy corners where the steel of a weapon might be pointing at them, gleaming; really (I thought, not without compassion), they saw themselves through the worn-out eyes of their guests and said to themselves, feverishly: The span of our life is drawing to a close, why so fast, don't we still have so much to take and to give.

I left quickly, because I did not have the courage to speak to the

Bastiers as I should and because I wanted to deliberate before I spoke directly to Marie Sachs.

That night I sent her this message:

You expose yourself like you assume Maria Martinez was forced to. You know that what they said about her will necessarily never be said about you, so what's the meaning of it? Your audience doesn't know anything about the woman who painfully, fiercely inspires you—and so what? I don't find this unpleasant, but what's the point? What are you trying to make me understand?

But in the middle of all these elegant, fresh, and gracious women with alabaster shoulders could be seen a Negress of the most beautiful variety, Señora Maria Martinez, a singer in a rather new genre, nicknamed "the Malibran of Havana," her homeland. Also a favorite of Queen Isabella and under the protection of the Duchess of Valence in Paris. This singular artist is between twenty-six and twenty-eight years old. She represents the most perfect African type: skin of a dazzling black with fiery glints, a high and supple waistline, magnificent arms, ivory teeth, scorching gaze. We knew that she was supposed to sing; I ask you whether the curiosity was kept alive. I have not said anything of Señora Martinez's dress, which I found shocking. Imagine a sumptuous pink brocade outfit in the latest style of Parisian fashion. A Negress dressed in brocade and in the Parisian style, is that not horribly out of sorts? But all that was soon forgotten. The Negress had taken up her guitar. She first

gave a vivid bolero with full African passion, then an Arabic melody, something incredible, dreamlike, impossible, a kind of drama that lent an unknown strange and fantastical character to the black singer's voice, to her gestures, her guttural accents, her ardent movements, which made one shudder with pleasure.
—*Revue étrangère de la littérature, des sciences et des arts,* January 28, 1852

Tonight you too gave us something incredible, etc. How and why did Maria Martinez become your model, I would love to be able to answer that question, it would greatly help me, for my part, to get to work.

I spent the rest of the night reading over again the file that I had created on the topic of Maria Martinez. I was so perfectly familiar with each sentence that, though acting as though I was reading, I was really reciting, just as, if I were religious, I would have recited a prayer I had known since childhood.

Then, at dawn, feeling not fatigue but rather an unfamiliar kind of exultation, not cynical and desperate but on the contrary oddly joyful, I wrote these first lines:

Maria Martinez was born in Havana, around 1825, of parents who were not slaves though they were of African origin. At only a few years old, little Maria sang so remarkably and was such a natural at the guitar that a Spanish soldier, Aguilar y Conde, who happened to hear her as he was strolling down the street, was immediately entranced by this child and decided to become her patron.

When Maria's parents died, Conde, who was meant to return to Spain, brought his protégée with him to Sevilla. He provided her with a solid musical education, such that Maria could later give lessons that would allow her to make a living as well as enter the Conservatory of Madrid, in order to round off her studies. Queen Isabella II took her under her protection. Maria sang regularly at court. She was so highly esteemed that she was encouraged to leave for Paris; there she would reveal the extent of her gifts, the excellence of her training.

That same day, though Marie Sachs had not responded, I sent her another message, slightly embarrassed to admit that I was disappointed by her silence, even though, a few weeks earlier, I had wished nothing more than to never have anything more to do with that woman.

How intelligent, charming, personable Maria Martinez must have been since childhood, to spontaneously inspire in so many important people the desire to help and support her, a desire that had certainly not arisen from the fact that Maria Martinez was black, but that, to the contrary, found a means of arising and expressing itself in spite of that fact.

Then I quoted for Marie Sachs an excerpt from an article that had appeared in *Le Musée des familles* (1851–1852):

> For the past two months, society's finest members have not been able to stop discussing the Black Malibran, the Queen of Spain's original artist. Following the Viscount of Arlincourt, Madame Aguado, and Madame de Tascher, the new senators, ministers, and ambassadors have all opened their salons to the Negress, whom the Court of Madrid will soon jealously

call back. Everyone wants to see and hear this peerless and incomparable virtuoso.

Marie Sachs replied immediately, in a tone that seemed to me uniquely detached, as if, I thought with a blush, she had somehow grown bored of me.

She said that, if her own interest for Maria Martinez did not have to be explained, since it was natural and even inevitable, coming from a black artist, she did not yet understand what motivated me—why did I care about the life of Maria Martinez, her joys and her troubles, how did such a life concern me so deeply that I was that committed to bringing her to light and, above all, to burying myself in her—that nest of cold ashes?

No analysis, no inquiry, no inventive miracle could make me understand what the excerpts I was sending her and the words I had doubtless already written—adding vain and hollow phrases to older expressions, some more abject, some less—obviously did not reveal: What kind of person was Maria Martinez?

How did she suffer, how much distress did it cause her to endure setbacks and snubs with such stoicism; and when she was happy, proud, when she was receiving compliments or when the sound of her own voice seemed perfectly in tune and beautiful to her own ears, what form did her joy take?

Marie Sachs, for her part, claimed she did not want to know. What pretention, then, on my part!

She ended by declaring (in earnest? how to interpret this?) that all that was left for me to do was to take her, Marie Sachs, as the subject of my work, my curiosity, my fervor, and my affection.

She clarified that I would have to treat my model, that is, herself, with as much humility and gentleness as she devoted to her own patronage of Maria Martinez and, in addition, to accept that such an enterprise would elapse over the course of a whole life, hers or mine.

To conclude, she said she would meet me that evening by the Porte de la Chapelle, a neighborhood that I rarely visit and where, to be honest, I would have refused to go after nightfall had I not had such a strong desire to respond to this challenge by Marie Sachs, who had vaguely wounded, offended, but also, in a way, roused me.

The address that she had given me, at the base of a tall building, was that of a dreary, run-down bistro: drab tulle curtains, grimy windowpanes, a ragged awning.

A handful of customers scattered about the dirty tables were looking toward the back of the room, which at first appeared to be dark and empty until all at once I discerned Marie Sachs, standing and holding her curious little guitar a bit stiffly, her head lowered.

As if my entrance signaled the start of the show (as if the artist had been waiting for me), a bare lightbulb at the end of a string lit up above her.

I sat down on the edge of a chair, just next to the door, feeling uncomfortable.

I feel so ill at ease in such filth, such wretchedness, amid such sorrowful, silent scarcity.

There was no reason, I said to myself, for me to voluntarily go somewhere just to feel ill at ease.

I had resolved to get up, to leave, when Marie Sachs began to play her instrument.

I began watching her then, closely.

She was wearing a white robe that went down to her ankles. I noted that the dress must have once been very beautiful, very lovely.

Now it was an old rag studded with stains, torn in several places.

Marie Sachs's feet were bare.

The untidy ball formed by her hair, crossed by strands of unequal length, was pricked here and there by cloth flowers.

> As for the attire, we find that a ballgown is not at all appropriate for a black woman; that flowers, in what one might call her hair, have a rather clumsy effect.
> —*L'Argus*, June 21, 1850

When she lifted her head, overwhelmed by the blinding white light of the bulb, Marie Sachs gave off an air of extreme fatigue.

Her skin was gray, dull, riven with marks—from collisions, from blows, from falls?

She tried to speak or sing, gave up, and began again to play, then tried once more to make a sound, once more without success.

She had not managed to emit more than a hoarse squeak that, in another context, I would have taken for a cry of terror.

She made a vague, apologetic smile, her feet slipped on the tiles that must, I thought, be quite cold, she went to take a few steps, a dance of simultaneous exhaustion and extreme grace, then she played a few tunes, so merry, with such a light hand, so alert and with what seemed to me to be such virtuosity that I could not stop myself from laughing inside, under the simple effect of sudden and naïve pleasure.

Around me, the other patrons were smiling too.

She had literally lightened us up.

But the skinny frame, the ravaged face of Marie Sachs conveyed such poor health, such melancholy, such suffering that any sense of mirth soon left me.

And the more her music grew ardent and allegro, the more the infinite sorrow of the situation discomfited me—this watering hole, this neighborhood, the odor of failure, of illusory expectations, I felt on the verge of tears.

Hadn't I too, even if more subtly, failed in life?

But how important is failing or succeeding, when one doesn't suffer too much?

And by what yardstick can that be measured?

Suddenly one of the guitar's strings broke.

Surprised, Marie Sachs mewled again like a paltry, wounded little critter.

All liveliness left the room and no one who entered at that moment would have sensed even an echo of it.

Then Marie Sachs sneezed loudly.

I fled.

Returning up the Boulevard des Maréchaux, I wept with rage, with consternation.

I stopped cold, in the crush of traffic, in all that horror of life on the urban margins, to send a message to Marie Sachs.

My fingers went feverishly over the keyboard, I made mistakes that I didn't bother to correct.

Yes, yes, yes, I wrote to her, as if shouting, *I know that we suffer when we learn how short Maria Martinez's time of glory was, how quickly she slipped from success and respect to the greatest dereliction, I know that you think that her fate would have been less unfortunate if she hadn't been black—but,* I cried in my message, *can't we imagine that, as a white woman, she would have reached no triumph with her disconcerting songs, her original act, the general eccentricity of her character?*

She had to be black, I said to Marie Sachs, *for her particular talent to be appreciated, that way she was judged less as a woman than as a phenomenon, isn't that better?*

But yes, I have known the sadness of reading this:

> What a subject for an elegy, that poor Señora Martinez, who was first introduced to us under the pompous name of "the Black Malibran," and who today is reduced to begging for her guitar, seized with all her personal effects! With due justice it was turned over to her, an instrument for her labor, that is (euphemistically) her bread-and-butter!
> —*Revue et gazette musicale de Paris,* December 25, 1859

And that harrowing letter from Maria Martinez, do you know of it?

> I am in great distress, out of your kindness I request, Minister,
> assistance from the artists' fund in order to pay for my lodgings,
> where all my personal effects are being held.
> Believe me, Minister, such assistance shall never be given or
> received with more gratitude than by
> Your very humble and respectful servant
> Maria Martinez

And then this, in a letter written by Baudelaire:

> Did you know that the unfortunate Señora Martinez has been
> trundling around the pleasure cafés, and that a few days ago
> she sang at the Alcazar?
> —Charles Baudelaire, *Lettres 1841–1866*, Paris, Société du
> Mercure de France, 1906

*You know very well, I said to Marie Sachs, that these are old stories and that
they cannot be tempered, they cannot be undone.*
    Why, then, suffer for her still?
    What kind of justice are you granting her, supposing that she never got it?

I asked her then who she was, she, Marie Sachs, what kind of childhood she'd had, in what kinds of places, and if she felt that someone should make her merits, her courage, her talent known, thus repairing, perhaps, an indelible wrong.

Back home, I waited for a response until late that night.

But I never had any more communication with Marie Sachs, neither in person nor via the web, which I plumbed avidly over the next few weeks.

That night, in the frantic anticipation of any sign from Marie Sachs, I had written:

The name of Maria Martinez disappeared completely from the cultural sections of the newspapers and reviews only a few years after she had landed with a splash. What happened to her? At what age, under which conditions, where and how did she die? Did she work until the end, singing, dancing, playing? In what wretched state did she find herself, at the end? How poor, how destitute did she likely become when all was said and done?

The questions reveal little.

But they do tell of fear and awe, of incurable concern for a woman who disappeared in times and places that we can no longer explore, no hope of ever finding her again.

How, oh how we should like to take her into our arms, to protect her, this valiant woman who is also, in some way or another, doubtless abused and despoiled.

We can only clutch at her own perception, which is not a comforting one—it is under cover of its solitude that the feral cat survives.

As boats

and buses

go by

Yi SangWoo

Translated from Korean by Emily Yae Won

Past elongated drainpipe rusted ladder and whirring box fans up the side of a shabby building casting oblique shadow at its own feet, walk back down the street that's gleaming with a sky and sea fused into a single block from the light seeping through two distant narrow walls then down another side street that gives onto the sloping uphill path and there craning at building signs on either side of the incline Thien falls asleep on the stairs. You're always nodding off and in the same spot too, what's up with that, the aunties used to ask. Because sometimes I say and imagine things in my mind and I'm afraid you'll hear, for there had been two aunties, twins, at the noodle shop where Thien once worked and where as steam wafted up from pots Thien would confuse the memory of the gentle breeze blowing through the small window overlooking the alley and glimmering under creased eyelids with the future. Scenes Thien had seen somewhere and somewhen but which where and which when, Thien and the aunties who'd wipe the sweat away when Thien's own hands were occupied with soapy dishes meeting in the hall during breaks to watch TV or heading outside stretching limbs to share a smoke in the alley the sight of several

As boats and buses go by

hands damp and raw from washing veggies gesturing ring marks faded fingerprints softened nails dancing in the sun until the street brimmed with the light glancing off fingers images shimmering variously in front of the eyes right into the evenings when shift over Thien wandered the neighborhood alone. Walking past the low-roofed shoe repair shops where without fail old men sat stooped all the while holding onto the stories of And that's how Big Auntie's son wound up in prison or how Little Auntie the ballet dancer was trafficked at the age of twenty and had to live and work for two years abroad, as blue light soaked the edges of the dispersing dark of dawn and painted the windowpanes Thien would walk out to the harbor walk alongside as the passenger ships arrived and departed and on days when the view of the world passing by Thien's left cheek swirled with raindrops Thien would observe the line of people outside the immigration office and imagine lining up behind them and being interviewed for temporary residence. Papers at the ready cracking jokes with the immigration officer a white man finishes his interview with an air of annoyance while around him faces tense people rehearse lines numbered tickets in hand and these faces open up other faces locked away in memory faces that vanish the more one recalls them so get up resume walking before they evaporate for good. What brings you here. I arrived and found myself here. Turning into the side street with the cheap motel Thien would run into white women on their way to work long legs swishing eating doughnuts out of a box and they'd stand aside to let each other pass maybe share a word or a joke at other times pass in silence heads hung as low as the pits pocking their expressions and occasionally on days when Immigration's been hauling away anyone

As boats and buses go by

without a visa there is the retracing of steps over and over circling the park looping endlessly around the many bends that gird its unremarkable tower. Up the incline and down the decline the park full of forking paths look over the shoulder until look here comes oneself dressed as oneself in identical clothing and headed straight toward self only to stir awake and be met by sounds of slumbering from the next room where some have vanished overnight and those that managed to stay put were snoring as best they could to erase the humiliation and seated at the desk Thien would light a dangling cigarette as the aunties used to.

From the radio on board the ship a light jazz music flowed a so-called bay area sound as some passengers had once remarked saying how all port cities have a music channel devoted to fusion jazz. After making the safety announcement lowering the microphone passing the big window full of glittering sea Hara would head downstairs to

Lovers in matching denim jackets sit in an embrace whispering by the metro window head bowed the man opens and shuts his eyes from the depths of his lover's shoulder where his countenance remains buried murmurs gently as the woman's downcast gaze sidles over his eyelashes past the tails of his softly blinking eyes and behind her hair the orange glow of the tunnel as it collides with oncoming headlights fracturing their faces eyes noses lips veer off visages to the empty silence of the next carriage susurrations scattering to the winds in the rumbling of the oncoming metro broken lights in its wake and now as eyes misplacing loneliness lift up from the floor dark slops in from the window and beneath it two people no longer in an embrace sit each alone the break room for a round of cards or to catch a wink in the berth of a windowless cabin or to the mess just as lunchtime's ending only to leave the bland plate of Japanese curry rice unfinished. Star-shaped sugar granules unfurled white against the smooth dark coffee pale curls growing darker as they dissolved into the swirl of rippling black meanwhile two nuns in habits seated across from each other at the next table were looking out at the ocean blank spaces opening up now and then in the low thrum of their conversation as a long ray of sun swept over the sea and sliced through the mess blanching curry-stained white trays and coffee cups and shattered the darkened nodding profiles of passengers to shards. Returning plate and tray Hara headed outside past the faces now turned away from the view toward each other past the two conversing nuns and upon exiting the mess with brows knitted lips sealed tight barely able to fold the specific emotion away into some recess of the body an emotion unexpectedly come to light in the sun's blaze Hara stumbled back to the radio room and resumed the announcements. Listing in usual intonation and accent the dinner hours the onboard entertainment the event hours the time remaining to their destination until a calmness set in allowing Hara to fake smile at the silly antics of colleagues their attempts to make Hara laugh while on air, calm where there had been vertigo the mind free-falling in exact proportion to the exact reach of the sun's rays now all but forgotten. A small carton of milk a soboro bread to fuel the write-up of the ship's log before strolling the still-jazzy corridors humming along to the muzac pausing to flatten against the wall each time someone in cleaning uniform passed by with the laundry cart. Afternoons mornings nights Hara

As boats and buses go by

would wander the corridors long after the cleaners had come and gone leaning against the wall with arms crossed or head bowed humming a tune from childhood. Singing snatches of the song pausing starting up again in an undertone pausing again. Punctuating the near-chanting and singing of the words, a silence of Hara's own making to defy the void.

A handful of students in school uniforms were running along the beach. Bare feet encrusted in sand treading empty sky over rowdy footprints as shouts and laughter rang out leaping forward to envelop embrace the neck of the person up ahead hopping on each other's backs jumping in place long strands of hair aflutter wild spray of water spiraling up their knees now scampering back face-to-face with the person behind dropping their jaws simultaneously to scream fingers gleaming at either end of their outstretched arms ties loosened around shirt collars glimpses of bare necks and with skirt pleats flattened a handful of students in uniform were running along the beach. Bare feet encrusted in sand treading empty sky as shouts and laughter rang out over rowdy footprints jumping in place long strands of hair aflutter wild spray of water spiraling up their knees embracing necks hopping on each other's backs a handful of students were running along the beach. Jumping in place long stands of hair aflutter wild spray of water reaching up their knees scampering back face-to-face with the person behind fingers gleaming at either end of their outstretched arms ties loosened around shirt collars spray of water leaping forward to envelop embrace the neck of the person up ahead hopping on each other's backs dropping their jaws to scream scampering back face-to-face with the person behind fingers gleaming at either end of their simultaneously

Taking the escalator from the top floor of the department store building where the floors by design form a single corridor that unfurls all the way down to the ground floor, watching people saunter from one shop to another. Across white marble floors punctuated by chattering groups and the occasional solitary stroller Thien would stare at any face that looked forlorn even in company then realizing what was sought was a familiar expression would hurriedly turn away and look at the ceiling and see reflected off the silver mirror there a face rent along the shape and pattern of the mirror. The faceless rearview of all who had been walking sitting standing splintering then vanishing out of sight. A cloyingly sweet smell of flour hung in the chill air over the skating rink while Thien sat next to some kids eating corn dogs watched the Zamboni and the woman driving it wondered how long she'd worked here what her name was what she thought about as she smoothed the sheet of ice whether she liked noodles whether Thien could get a job driving a Zamboni Are you waiting for someone, asked a child who'd eaten the batter clean off the dog.

outstretched arms and swinging loosened ties a handful of students were running along the beach. Flattened skirt pleats bare feet encrusted in sand treading empty sky over rowdy footprints jumping in place long strands of hair aflutter as wild spray of shouts and laughter rang out spiraling up their knees leaping forward to envelop embrace the neck of the person up ahead hopping on each other's backs dropping their jaws to scream drops of water gleaming at either end of their outstretched arms now scampering back face-to-face with the person behind bare feet encrusted in sand treading empty sky over rowdy footprints leaping forward the bare neck of the person up ahead flattened skirt pleats as Thien searched for words the Zamboni exited the rink and imagining the child who still hadn't finished the corn dog hurriedly waddling behind the other kids Thien sat by the side of the department store skating rink where no one ever struck up a conversation. Much like the view falling away even as Thien's eyes passed over it or passed from forlorn faces to ceiling mirror a brief sideways glance while Thien leaned forehead on window glistening with rain picked out an employee reading beneath the sandwich shop's awning head covered in hairnet hand in uniform pocket a scene that promptly melted away under the gleam of bright lights rain spattering the bus as the vehicle leaned into a curve Thien staring on at faces on buses passing to and fro in the next lanes eyes fixed on windowpane until the faces slid down borne on rainwater suffused with the glow of streetlights traffic

Why aren't you in skates? I only mean to sit here My mum does that too Do you like to skate? Yeah I do but also I don't Sometimes I want to go home but I've no choice Why not? This is a secret but actually the world's about to dry up entirely you know and that means I'll be the last kid who's ever ice skated How did you figure that out? I had a dream where the sea had turned into desert and grown-ups were wandering the desert crying and crying At first I thought the grown-ups were just grown-ups but after I woke up I thought well that could be me It could right? Couldn't it? Aren't you cold? Do you want to eat my corn dog? No I'm fine you go ahead and enjoy it You smell of cigarettes I'm sorry Will I smoke too when I'm older? Well that depends on you So who are you waiting for? No one I'm here on my own Yeah I really need time to be on my own too Where d'you come from? From the roof garden No I meant which country are you from lights illuminated signage. Already past several sloping streets yet no matter where they happened to be passing and though it remained unseen there was the palpable sense of being enveloped by sea as though they were underwater and the bus entirely engulfed as drops of rain borne aboard by each new passenger traced their paths along the floor with each turn or tremor of the bus a single flower swaying atop the backpack of a woman who'd just boarded the stem longer than the length of the bag and Thien along with the rest of the passengers adrift in light slopping through glass and words streaming out of the radio each together gazed upon the pink bloom hovering over the stranger's back.

Stirred awake while trying to free a crushed arm Hara tossed and turned in search of a comfortable position before climbing down the berth taking care not to disturb sleeping colleagues. Walking down the corridor straight into the high wind blowing in off a sea glutted with night Hara looked up to see ghostly breath diffusing over a vast expanse of nocturnal cold stars glinting and beneath it the deck empty deserted. Even the late-night bar was shrouded in darkness and hovering by its bottle-lined windows a whiff of sick now mixing with the briny smell overflowing onto the deck lapped at Hara before subsiding. Clothes flapping about in wrinkled patters as dictated by gusts Hara turned to light a cigarette but the blast of air was overpowering and leaning against the rail Hara not out of interest in locating where the waves originated but merely needing to gaze out at something to keep the mind blank followed the wave beyond the wave beyond the wave swell and grow right there on the edge of night until there was no stuck fast hands flying up to cover the face Hara stood in this way waiting until the safety of darkness pooled in the cupped hands allowing the sighing out of expletives once more. Wandering two floors of underground corridors in search of a lighter not a single soul to be encountered so down to the lower storage floor where Hara had never ventured before at this time of night and there at the end of the corridor a sliver of light beneath an open door.

Could I trouble you for a light? Yeah sure, the person in cleaning uniform handed over a lighter and returned to their book. On night duty are you. No. This is the only time I can focus on reading. You mean you come here to read every day at this hour? That's right. Good thing we arrive early tomorrow morning. Hmn. Not so sure. Not sure? Yes. I don't actually disembark. Why not? I don't have a visa. Handing back the lighter with a fresh cigarette to say thank you Hara waved away the smell of urine that had begun to waft over from the piles of washing as the cigarette unfurled, Is it good what you're reading? Yeah it's good. What is it? Just a novel. I don't think I read a single book after I turned twenty. Not like it's necessary. So why do you read? Dunno. Maybe I need new pasts. Why on earth would you need that? The past makes me sick to my stomach. I see. It seems they're constantly

smoke left to breathe out then stood flush against the wind as it swept past and through the body and back and only then as a sensation of emptiness took hold as if the heart cavity had been hollowed out finally looked away. Tasting blood where lips had torn from a cigarette

Under a light bulb swaying to and fro in rhythm with the ship the storage room was piled high with laundry and amid unwashed linen someone wearing a cleaning uniform sat reading a book.

readying to pull me under. I'd rather be curious about the future. I want to get there asap. The two of them sit on the piles of washing their knees not quite touching, What do you imagine you'll find there? The most amazing cocktails and beaches. Handsome puppies and amazing buildings too probably. After hours of swimming at the beach with the handsome dog we'd come back to find a wash-and-dry machine that automatically cleans us up and dries us off. Maybe there'll be a laser sword as well. What would you want that for? What do you mean what for, to cut off the dick of any bastard that tries it on me. After which I'll shove another guy's head into the hole. Like. Like a centaur? No like a human caterpillar. Never heard that one before. What about you? How do you imagine the future? Hmm. I've always found it strange, but the more I try to remember the more my memories seem to vanish. Like. Like they're empty? One thing at least is clear. What's that? That then or now I have nowhere to land. Don't be like that. It'll work out. I'm merely stating the truth. It's the only thing I remember clearly. We escaped from civil war and spent nearly two months roaming the desert before border patrol caught us and sent us here. To this ship you mean? No. To this era. I don't follow. I mean the closer I get to where I'm from memories of it naturally fade away. Where are you from? I'm from the future.

Frail and slant the stacked sunlight glides down the entire length
of the alleyway to lift off at the shore, and there in the street stood a
child. Meeting Thien's eyes the child turned away the bleached white ray
obscuring her face from Thien to whom Big Auntie introduced the child
as the daughter of her imprisoned son. Keeping one eye on the child as
she wandered the alley all three were busy cooking noodles while one

the child installed herself on a vacated seat with an orange-flavored ice pop while they gathered around the plastic table in the alley, How about an outing on our next day off, Little Auntie saying I'll bring lunch Big Auntie saying Never mind that let's splurge on lunch for once Yes Let's Thien and Little Auntie clapping as twilight extended its branches between the narrow crevice of walls past the applause and the three faces to envelop the child unwittingly swinging her legs in the empty space between feet and floor. That night Thien wrote a letter. No soul to send it to more in hopes that the memory of writing it rather than its actual contents would remain and endure Thien jotted down the day's observations. The friend encountered on the way back to the motel. The difference in the friend's gait. How they'd been alone today whereas usually they were with someone else. How as each of them stood aside to make room for the other time had with only a shadow of doubt slithered past between them. The doodles left on the alleyway table outside the shop. The sneakers the child Thien met for the first time had been wearing. Some more people had been thrown out of the motel today the sound of snoring had waned.

or two customers doffed their fishing hats and sat down to gaze out the window the sound of breathing flowing across all their faces. Every free moment the aunties exchanged a few words with the child through the window would even go out into the alley to play the quiet child's voice ringing out in laughter at their goofiness at which Thien laughed but then meeting the child's eyes unfailingly looked away. Once the customers who had sat dozing as though in a stupor their glasses of lukewarm beer forgotten on the table had stirred and gone

As promised the aunties and Thien met outside the bookshop. The child wasn't there. The mother had come back to fetch her. Wandering through streets lined with secondhand bookshops the aunties seemed to find the outing a nuisance now that it was happening and tagging behind Thien saw how their backs were more face-like than their actual faces more telling and here and there construction sites blue canvas tents flapping like waves crashing along the shore a bakery on the ground floor of yet another tented building here they stopped for bread then passed the noises creeping from shuttered doorways three or four printing houses a hole-in-the-wall stationery shop the two still in front scarves aflutter two women twins with dark long hair long coats walking down stone stairs. Barely looking at the other brushing aside coat fronts to thrust their hands in the pockets of high-waisted trousers or stroking the belt of their coat their gaze light as a breeze on the street where gingko leaves startled underfoot and people sat legs crossed at sidewalk tables drinking their teas coffees and the aunties passed by looking off in different directions scattering a handful of words as if answering without answering asking without asking while to one side the quiet sea gleamed from time to time before vanishing blazing back into view up the sloping path leading to an old wall cracked by time arms nearly brushing sidling collapsing connecting the distance between them to the wide-open space atop the hill catching their breath they leaned elbows against the railing of the observation point Thien noticing how their faces were like everyone else's beyond the railing over which they now looked as the pair turned and headed back toward Thien their hair scattered white like the light of the sun. The three sat down on a bench to share the bread

As boats and buses go by

they'd bought, Shouldn't be picky about bread should try them all, as they launched into tales of the latest letter to have arrived from the son in prison the choir class Little Auntie's been attending which of their regulars at the noodle place goes back the longest all the way back to when they were refugees displaced by war and Thien listened concerned or laughing but not sharing in the telling as the two aunties tapped at their sore knees with their fists. And though the granddaughter was not mentioned the two aunties followed any passing child intently with their eyes until the child had passed out of view and when it was time to go Big Auntie handed a book she'd bought earlier and Small Auntie flowers as gifts for Thien.

In the gloaming boats ships floated amid a patchwork of leaves and boughs and in a corner saturated the exact hue of blue as the waters below a man in Navy uniform practiced his horn. Poorly a beginner notes all tangled as firecrackers shot by students on a school trip lit up pale insipid around him and across the beautiful nighttime park while wind roved over the hill shaking barbed wire fences sea and sky fusing as if by suction into a dark gloom settling over various faces their expressions mislaid

Person on the edge of a bed removing a sweater. Light entering window through curtains hands at waist peeled blue sweater up inside out over flesh-colored flesh marked by outline of underwear hair clinging to nape of neck bare shoulder line faintest rash near shoulder blades coffee-stained sheets sound of car horns shadow passing over head in darkened bedroom wrists bound in sweater arms expelled a thin sigh as shoulders heaved person on the edge of a bed removing a sweater. Hands at waist peeled blue sweater up inside out over flesh-colored flesh marked by outline of underwear bare shoulder line hair clinging to nape of neck faintest rash near the shoulder blades through curtains light-stained sheets sound of car horns passing over darkened bedroom casting shadow wrists bound in sweater arms expelled a thin sigh as bed heaved person on the edge of a bed removing a sweater. Through curtains sound of car horns hands at waist peeled blue sweater up inside out over hair clinging to sheets bare shoulder line faintest rash near nape of neck coffee-stained flesh-colored flesh marked by burns airplane lights entering window passing over darkened bedroom wrists bound in sweater arms

As boats and buses go by

expelled a thin sigh as back heaved person on the edge of a bed removing a sweater. Hands at waist peeled blue sweater up inside out over trails marked by ships sailing over seas hair clinging to nape of neck bare shoulder line faintest rash near shoulder blades coffee-stained sheets sound of someone disappearing in darkened bedroom person on the edge of a bed both wrists bound in sweater arms

A dozen people in coalescing dusk spilled off the ship passengers crew alike Hara the last one to disembark looked around but too dark still for lights dotting the deck to show people in cleaning uniforms. Over the horizon clouds gradually tinting with bright blue rays of wind ruffled hair as Hara walked backpack over one shoulder of moleskin coat tying back loose strands and sensing colleagues beckoning from across the street hailed a taxi to leave the harbor. Eyes averted from their unpleasant joyless company doubtless Captain the first one off the boat making a beeline for the casino losing money while muttering his poor daughter's name in lieu of a prayer not realizing for a second that he's long been erased from his daughter's life Hara who received phone calls periodically from friends family whomever to exchange news pleasantries knew how to exclude company from life. Still blue the taxi windows reflected the passing bus full of dozing people swaddled in the depths of their thick winter coats their eyes closed and Hara peered at elderly faces their heads growing heavy only to see the face of the person who claimed to have come from the future, recalled the stir of emotion when they had then laughed it off as a joke. Sorry it's from the novel I'm reading now, the comment soon forgotten in silly banter but the truth remained that wherever that person was from there was nowhere they could disembark. Blocking out the old women on the bus who grew increasingly mute the longer one looked at them Hara waded into the hot water after a perfunctory shower and lay back with a warm wet towel draped over forehead steeped in the steam of the bathhouse and thought instead of groceries. Potatoes minced meat Thai chilies spinach onions curry powder low-fat milk frozen pizza beer also a certain person whose face remained faint this opaque person whose vague gestures and voice wouldn't come into focus looking out at the sea from the noodle shop like the people asleep on the bus or those for whom Hara had stood aside in corridors vanishing as they had into distant memory and who together with those places would never again resurface as Hara's body rigid from the cold and nervous tension slowly thawed in the warm water melting flowing to some far-off place eyelids slack then heavy as beads of water on the ceiling grew obscured. Snow was falling. Hara was sitting at the noodle shop. Two people who had walked in after Hara and had lingered awhile after their meal gazing silently out the window got up and left but Hara sat with elbows splayed on the table. The sound of wind rattling the windows eddied around with the smell of frying vegetables as Hara sat chin in one propped-up hand half-listening to pop music from the radio and said some music really good music was so freaking good you could die listening to it and Hara's mother plopped down the bowl of noodles and slapped Hara on the back. It's a figure of speech I don't actually want to die I just want to run away to this other dimension the music creates, but Hara's mother had walked out to the alley to let in the street cats and Hara blew on the bowl lifted it to sip at the hot broth first. Standing in the light snow drifting in the alley holding the small kittens that hadn't yet made it inside Hara's mother checked on the feeding bowls and beyond the profile of her face Hara glimpsed the ocean alongside Hara's own face reflected on the pane then resumed eating. As Hara was about to leave Hara's mother slipped a long-stemmed flower in the backpack asked Hara to bring it home but seeing how the flower jutted out past the flap it would be beyond embarrassing to walk around with that thing the shame of it bound to induce a panic attack rendering Hara unconscious or a swooning fall capped by fatal concussion but Hara's mother simply said thanks hon and half-nudged half-kicked Hara out of the shop that was alive with the yowling of cats.

Arriving at the bus station the clouds had brightened twilight was casting a slender insidious light over them as faces likewise washed clear and footsteps grown leisurely made the passing view appear to form pockets even as it flowed past. In the book you're reading what is the future like? Do you really want to know? It's all made-up anyway. Yes I want to know. Isn't the future itself made-up in the first place? Anything interesting? Well, in the future they replay the memories of people from olden days. How? There's a tiny chip which holds wave-forms of images extracted from the brains of dead people. You put that on the temple like so and it makes the brain waves vibrate and unfold the images in your head. They're so vivid it really feels like I'm there, like I live there. Is it like doing drugs? You could say that. People come together to sit or lie down and replay the memories over and over because these are anywhere between one and forty seconds long. The bus headed up the overpass spanning the immense width of the sea and out the windows to the left long buildings lined the fluent shore glittering from head to toe unveiled by sunlight tunneling its way out of the clouds past the unattainable fluency and the graphic-like buildings the bus climbed up the overpass arcing over the sea and out the window the space between sea and sky was dazzlingly empty the more one looked at it the more one felt emptied of breath as if extinguished from the here and now as orange light flooded the windows opposite. Turning back see the flower poking out of the bag. Backs of passengers steeped in glowing sunset. In this bus where light explodes forth like a series of exclamations a sense of déjà vu seen this before somewhere somewhen people wrapped in setting sun like this laughing gesturing talking but which where and which when as the gloam continued to deepen beyond closed eyes past the fluent shore graphic-like buildings and the bus climbed up the overpass and through its windows the space between sea and sky artificially empty the more one looked the more one felt emptied of breath as if extinguished from the here and now as orange light flooded in from the windows opposite. Turning back see the flower poking out of the bag. Backs of passengers steeped in glowing sunset. In the bus where light explodes forth like a series of exclamations a sense of déjà vu seen this before somewhen people who are erased in the blink of an eye no matter how luminous but which when and which people even as the gloam deepened beyond closed eyes past the fluent shore and as the bus climbed past the graphic-like

As boats and buses go by

buildings outside the window the fenestrate space between sea and sky

Dineo Seshee Bopape

Six paintings from *Convoluted Story*

Exhibited in 2020 in
response to "As boats
and buses go by"

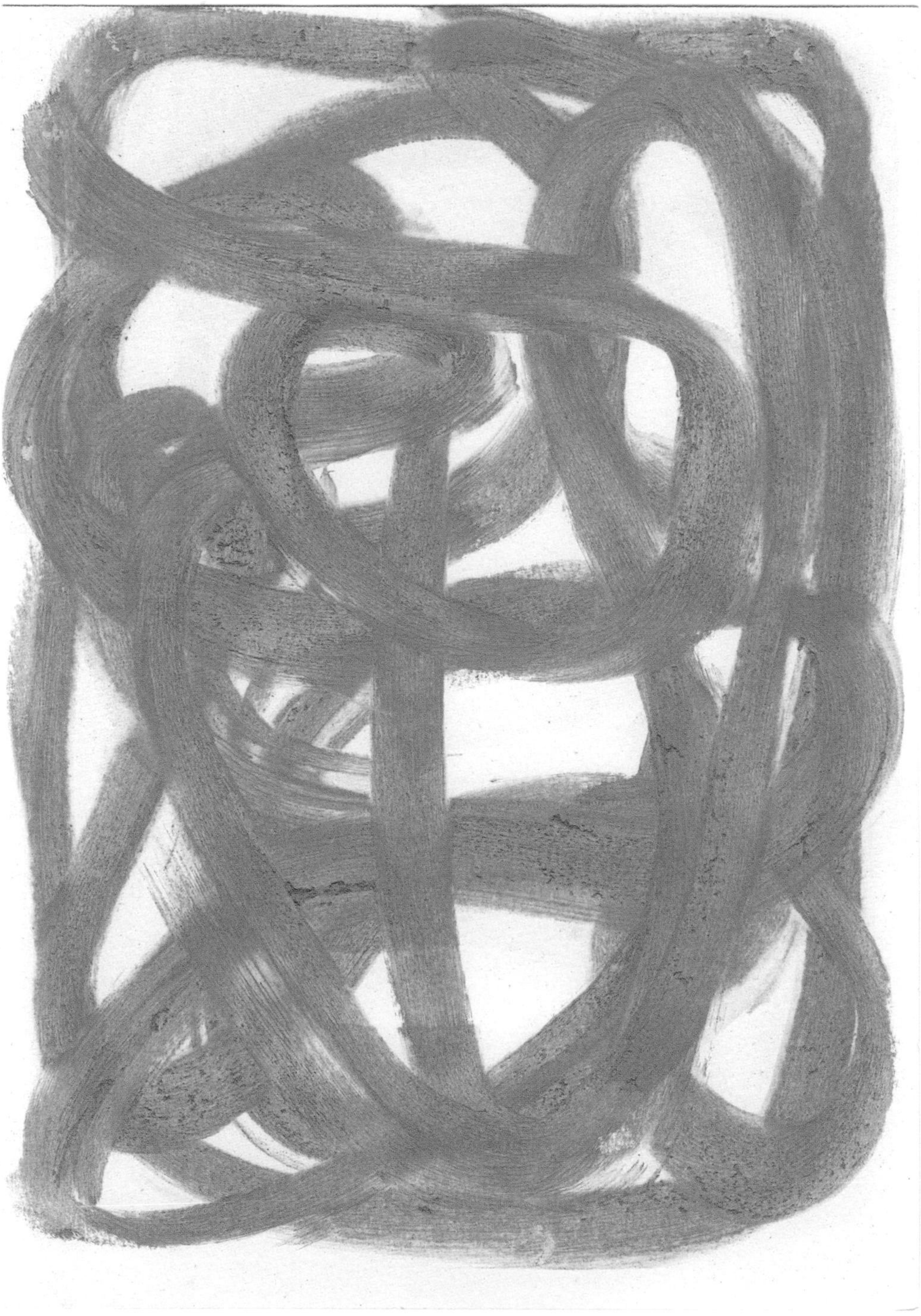

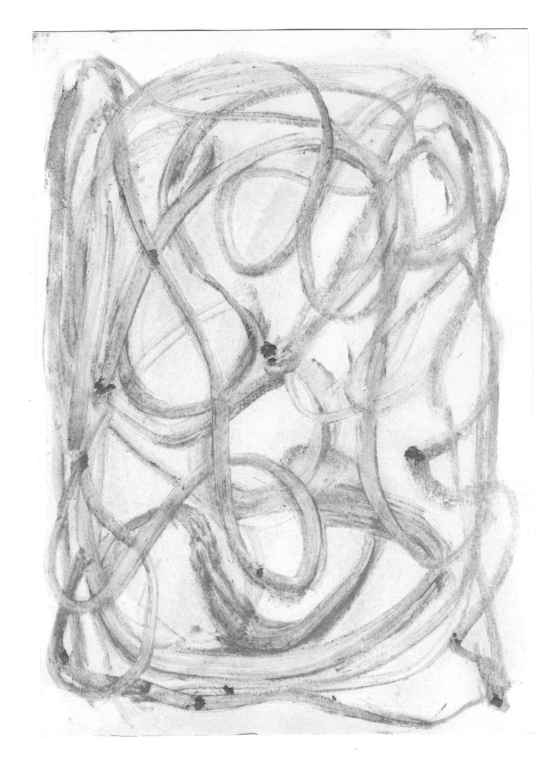

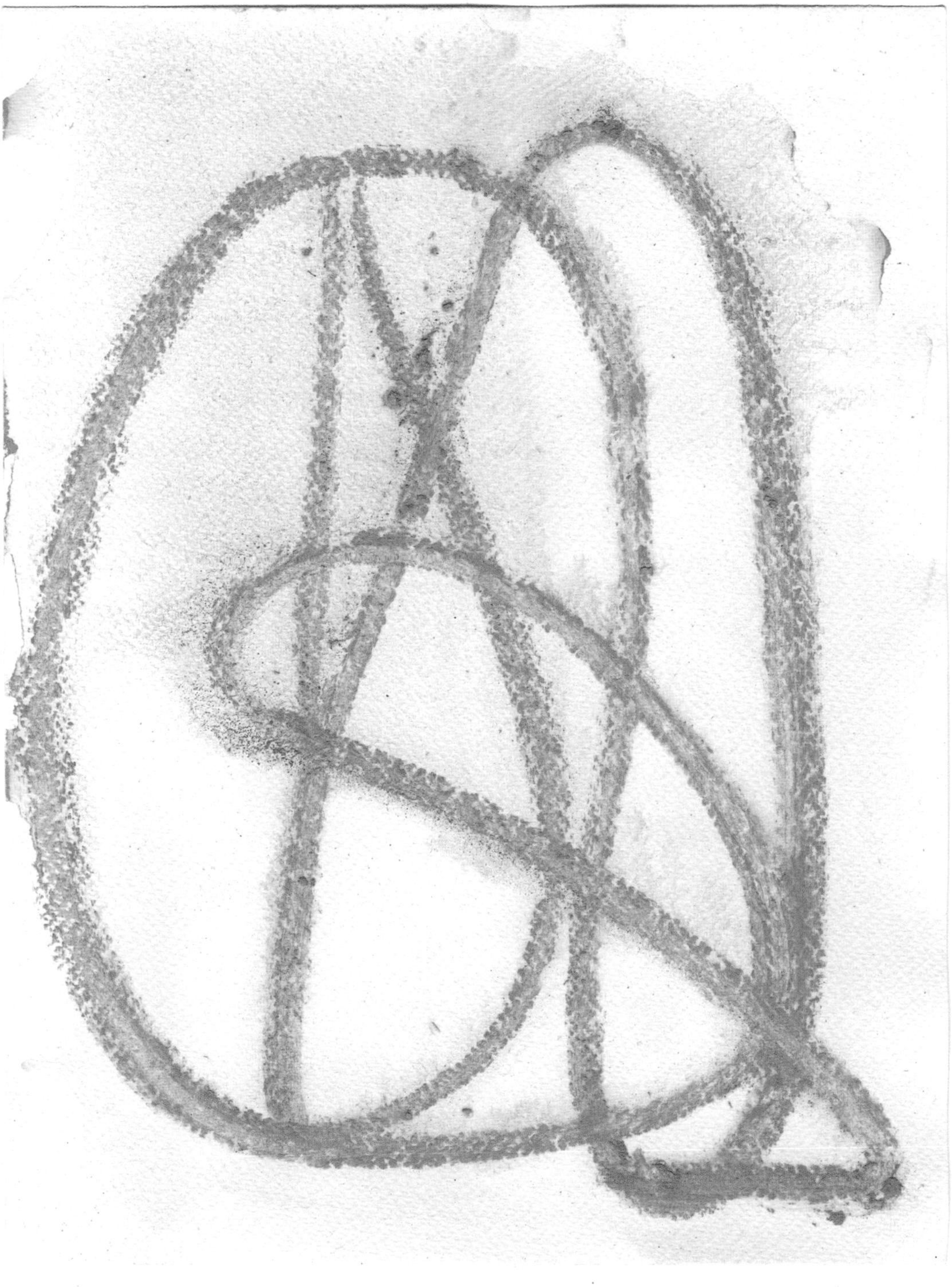

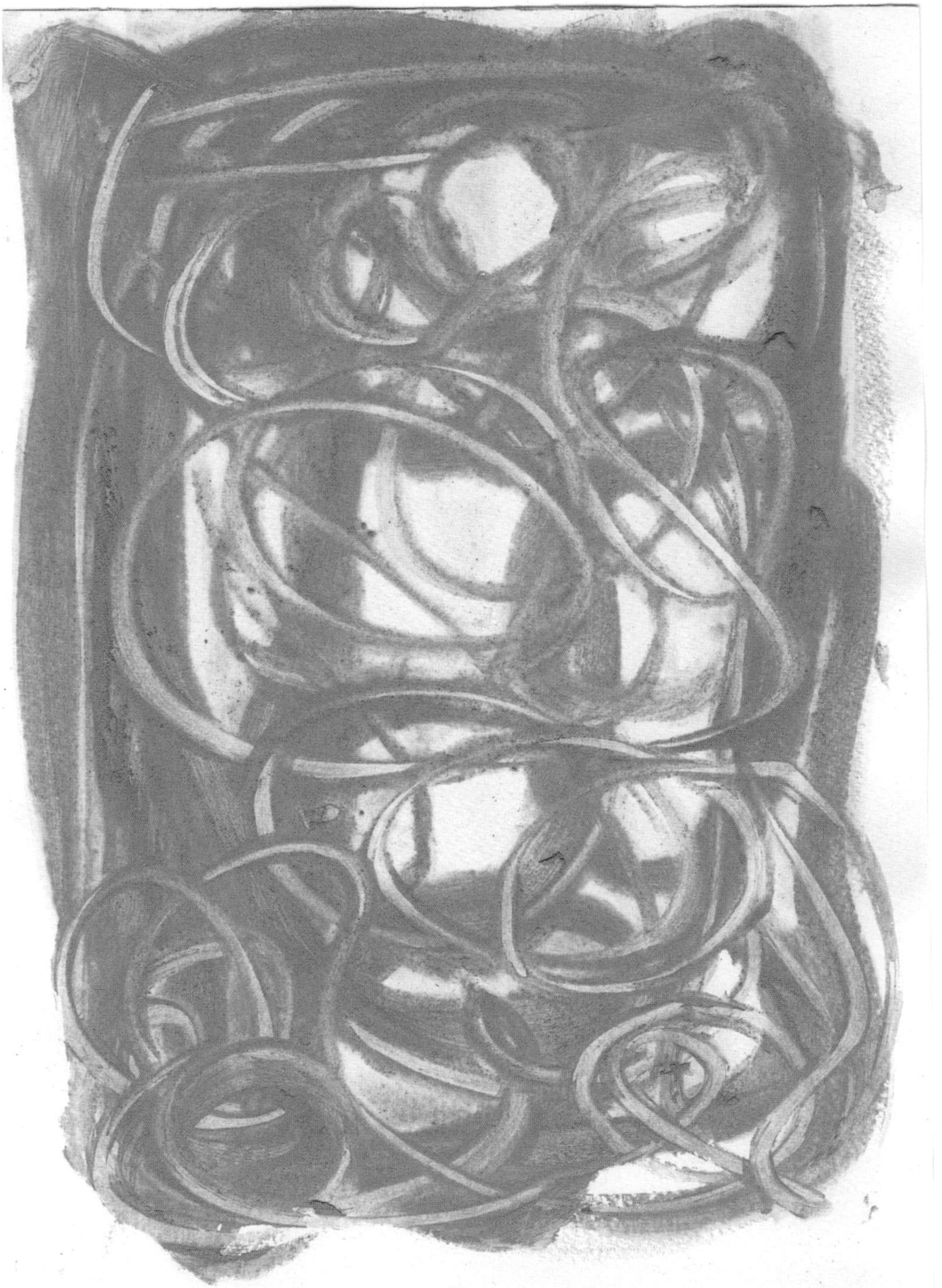

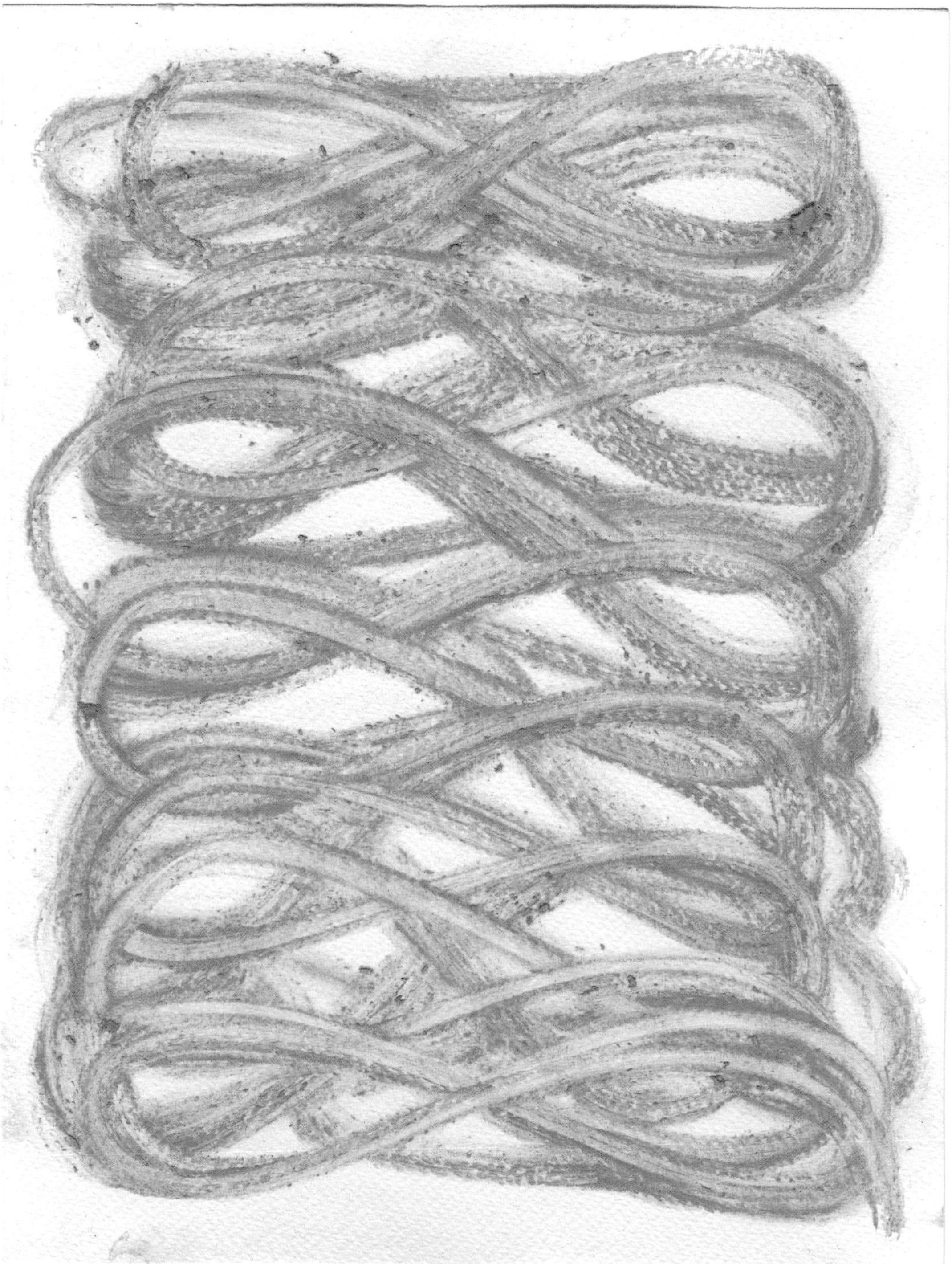

from

Closed

Window

Rodrigo Flores Sánchez

Translated from Spanish by Robin Myers

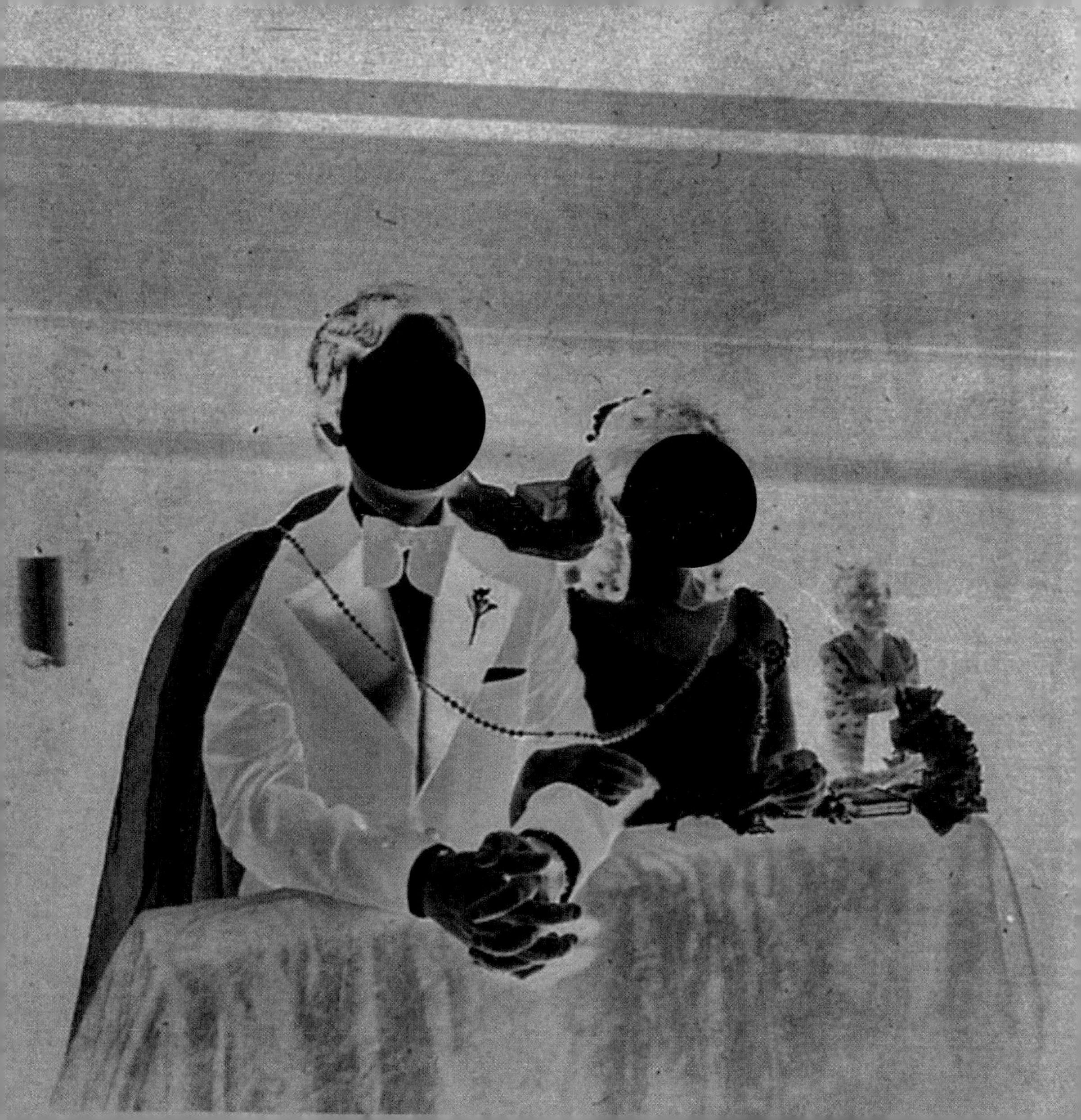

HUMAN MACHINE MOTHER
OF CHIMERA MOTHER
OF THE SPHYNX

Touch Me in the Morning

According to the Chinese zodiac
The year nineteen seventy-three was a special year
The Year of the Ox

Mexico held spotless presidential elections
The author of *Muerte sin fin* died
And *The Godfather* won the Oscar for Best Picture

That was the year Diana Ross released her fourth LP
The song that goes We don't
Have tomorrow but we had yesterday

It topped the charts
The song that goes Wasn't it me who said
That nothing good's gonna last forever

My parents weren't married yet

So their photo hadn't yet been torn
It's obvious right?

They married in nineteen seventy-five Year of the Rabbit
I have a black-and-white photo from their wedding
They gaze at the priest with devotion

Diana Ross was thirty-one
My parents couldn't yet have sung the song that goes
Let me watch you go with the sun in my eyes

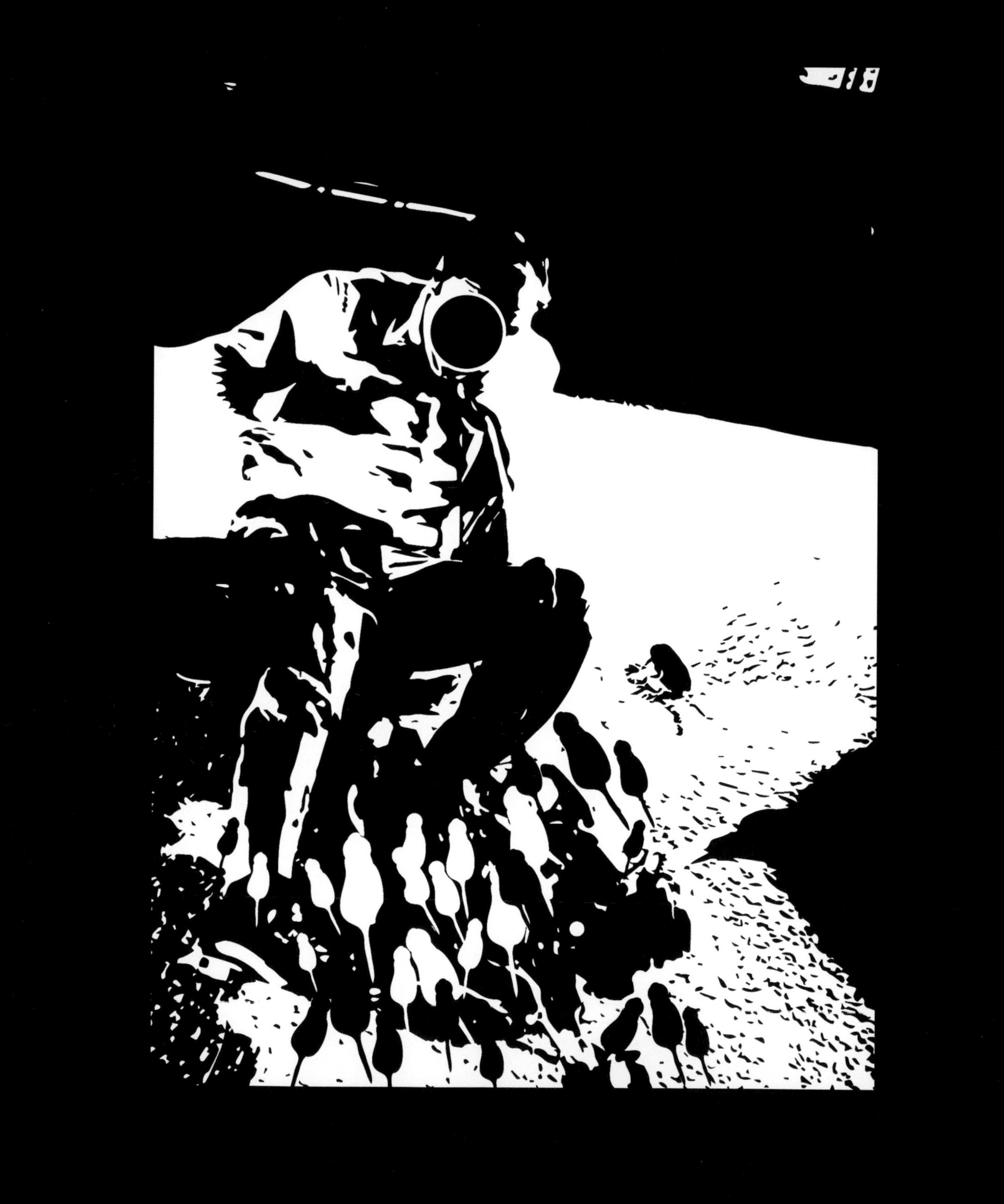

BY ATTACKING THE MANY-HEADED CREATURE
THE HERO DEVOURS
HIS OWN FAMILY

Rat Man

Another family portrait
A man is devoured
By rats

It's the image in a book
A book
Of movie stills

The devoured man is wearing a raincoat
And the rats swarm over what you see
The rats devour the man in the raincoat

You looked with panic and fascination Two sides
Of the same coin
I wear a raincoat and walk away

That photo

Is panic and vertigo and I don't know where the book is and I walk closer
Can I eat it? you ask

Touch it in the morning
And then just walk away Why
Do rats hunt our heads?

I've searched for the book, but I can't find it. It had a thick cover, as far as I can remember, but maybe I'm wrong. The book, in English, contained reviews of horror movies. I'd return to it again and again in the apartment where I lived then. I can see myself setting it down on the rug, opening it wherever the pages fell, and staring intently at the pictures for a few minutes. I couldn't make sense of the reviews, but I was transfixed by the photos, two in particular. Today, after nearly forty years, I still look at the face of a girl split by an axe and the figure of a man in a raincoat being eaten by rodents. Some images are difficult to forget; or, better put, they're recreated again and again in our memories. Some windows change shape.

For several minutes, sometimes hours, the portrait sitters would enter the lens. The shutter speed would be dilated to withhold a scrap of space. Then, during a torturous process, the silvered plates were iodized, the images registered in the camera obscura. These materials had to be turned over and over until it was possible to recognize, under proper lighting, a grayish image. Today, images with one hundred thirty-four million colors are automatic. The process has been simplified into a single click. Unlike before, models are expelled by the instant and deposited as bits into the creases of a cloud.

LIONS BOARS HYDRAS
LIVE
AND ROAR IN US

Celestial Bodies

I pinned thumbtacks
Into photos Into
the eyes of all the photographs

It was a strategy
To forget about myself or else
To shine a little

It must have been nineteen ninety-five
When I started college
In another Year of the Pig

I think
That's when I painted
My bedroom blue

I arranged photos like stars

I'm in a few of them
I remember an image

I'd finished
A sweaty race I pinned
Thumbtacks into my exhausted face

I profaned the images
To hide myself from them I
Described myself in opaque and brittle universes

I'm going to look for them I'll discover
Their glow
They must be around here somewhere

I'll find them in the drawer
Where I keep
Black holes

CREATING CONSTELLATIONS
OUT OF RUINED
BODIES

I've imagined photos that don't exist and many of my evocations have been sparked by images I appear in as a child and don't remember; both procedures are the implants of adulterated memories. Spirit photography was in vogue in the late nineteenth century. Prints were made onto preexisting daguerreotypes and untimely figures would emerge from the new images. For a while, the art of photography became a trap for ghosts. There's a photo of my brother as a baby. His pale face peers out of the white stroller. I think he got sick that day. It was Christmas and he was hospitalized a few days later. He nearly died. You can see he's crying in the photo, distressed I think. The ghost of illness is already present, although maybe I'm the one who's forging the memory by overexposing it and in that window there's nothing to see but someone demanding to be fed. Another possibility is that the image has nothing to do with this event and that my brother isn't my brother.

During World War II, the British Air Force devised a countermeasure to jam the German radars before bombing their positions. It was called Window. As part of Operation Gomorrah, a group of aircrafts under the auspices of Commander Arthur Harris deployed ninety million sheets of tinfoil, which protected the bombers from detection when their explosives blew the city of Hamburg to smithereens. Dropping windows like decoys was ultimately devastating to the German city, since the Luftwaffe was unable to identify the British planes. Wallace Stevens says that a poet must be able to abstract himself and also to abstract reality, which he achieves by situating reality in the imagination. In this sense, the poet's vocation involves not only resisting intimidation by the pressures of reality (that is, allowing himself to be seduced by those windows and their reflections despite the imminent bombardment of events), or not only bearing witness to the world's intrinsic devastation, but also remaining alert to the dazzling rainfall of mirrors and availing himself of tinted glasses in order to formulate a hypothesis about what he perceives and experiences. The survival of poetry at the margins of reality is impossible; it isn't even desirable. Nor is it possible to long for the confiscation of the poem's capacity to veil and reveal, or for, alternatively, the insertion of the news bulletin, the insipid vignette, the self-serving quip, the anecdote dressed in a minor dose of fatuous morality or the coveted love of truth, which tends to yield its antithesis: hypocrisy and indifference. Like old photographs, poetry, paraphrasing Stevens once again, may be nothing but the illumination of a certain surface in moments of darkness.

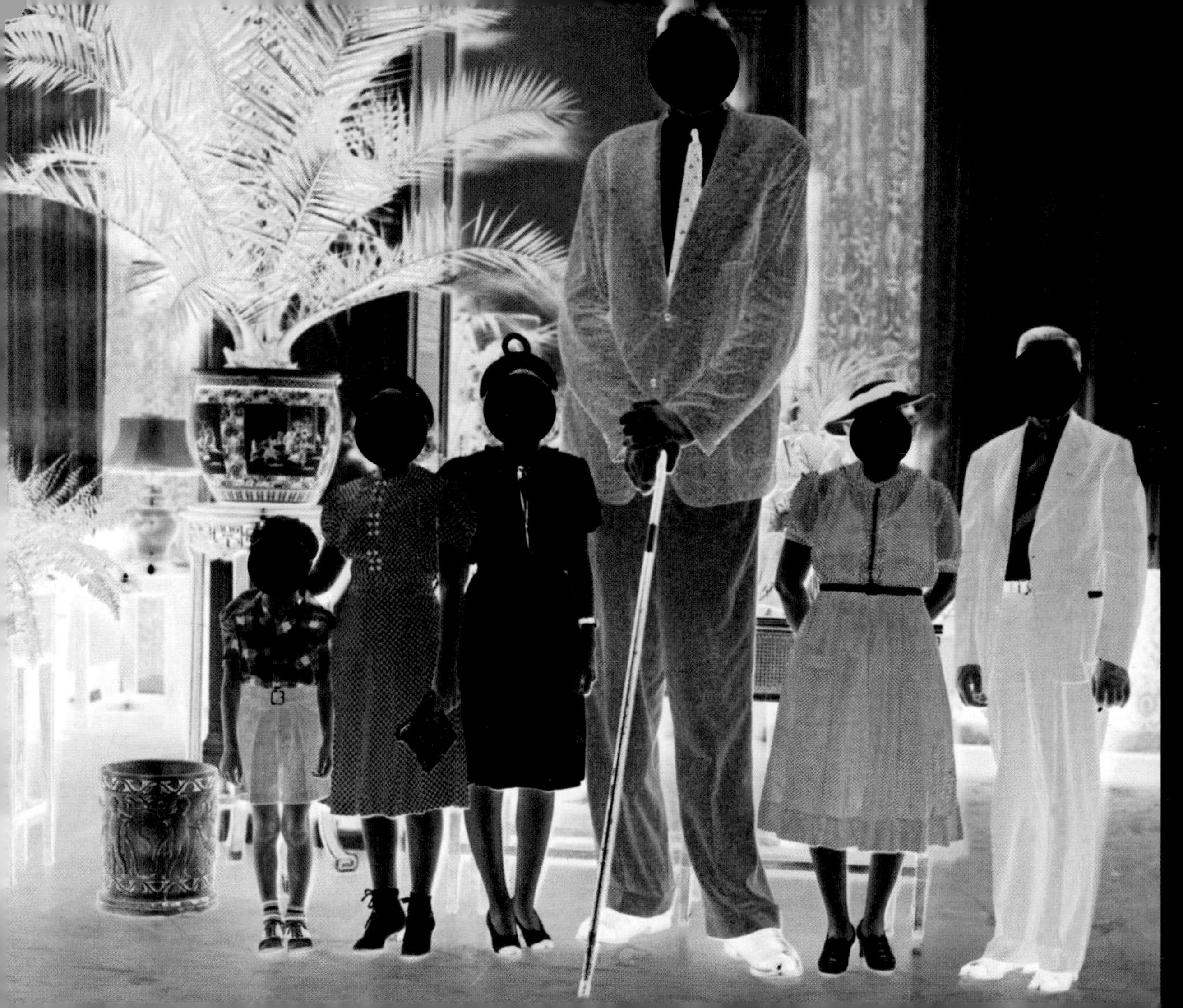

HE UTTERS
WORDS OF LOVE
AS HE COLLAPSES

Emotional Education

The tallest man in the world
Robert Wadlow
Was always smiling

His legs
Were fragile brittle bamboo stems
In photos he looks like he's collapsing

His parents exhibited him in circuses
He was almost ten feet tall
And died at the age of twenty-two

The longest-living woman in the world
Was a French citizen
Her face was a red raisin

After her death

The skin of her flat biography
Has stretched

It seems
She assumed her mother's identity
And corrupted the evidence

Marilyn vos Savant
Has the highest
IQ on record

She is the author of an uninspiring advice column
She is the epitome of a luminous intelligence
At the service of an edifying oeuvre

In Ask Marilyn
She confirms that emergency rooms
Are busiest on weekends

She asserts that the greatest number of gringos are born
On September sixteenth
And lightning bolts are zigzag-shaped

I acquired knowledge and sayings
Amid the curiosities
Of the record book

And since one thing leads to another
My morbid spirit
Broadened its horizons

Soon came other titles like *Mystics of the World*
Most Notorious Crimes
Weirdest Objects

I asked my dad to hide
These combustible materials
In hidden hiding-places

But the next night
I'd search their pages once again
With impatience and fruition

I was equally terrified
By *The Twilight Zone*
And *Unsolved Mysteries*

Then I took a shine
To the *Unusual Weekly*
I'd buy it at recess on Fridays

There were prototypical photos
The wedding of two incestuous siblings
Or a happy man beside a six-foot cricket

Around the same time
I started collecting installments
Of the *Crime Blotter*

The she-devil
The Boston Strangler
The case of Sharon Tate

These were my initiation readings
How strange
I was born in the Year of the Snake

INSIDE THE SWAMP
A VORTEX
BECKONS TO US

Frazer

On Wetar Island
There are shamans who cause illnesses
By harming shadows

On the Yukon River
An explorer
Prepares to take photos

Of people Of those
People who move
Who move happily among the huts

Folkloric glows
Unique documents
Picturesque portraits

But the village chief

Insists on peeking
Under the black cloth

At the sight
Of the figures traveling
Over the frosted glass

The spiritual reader
Prey to panic
Shouts

"He has all
Our shadows
Stuck inside the box"

Any act
Of reproduction
In part or in full

Of the images
In any form or medium
Is prohibited

As is any act of unauthorized
Dissemination
Or public communication

The Tepehuanes
Behold the camera
With deer-like fright

It takes five days
To persuade them
To be focused on

When they finally accept
They look like criminals
Before their execution

They believe that the photographer
Will steal their spirits
And feed on them

I meant to talk about myself But I ended up
Talking about The Golden Bough
Now I have a finger between my lips

from
The Pepper Forgers

Monika Sznajderman

Translated from Polish by Scotia Gilroy

The Boarding House of Memory

How do you feel now as they return: all these faces, events, and places? When, after more than seventy years, they come at night like thieves to steal your sleep and peace of mind? Until now, they've waited quietly, squeezed inside the waiting room of memory, but now they're running rampant.

It began three years ago with a letter from the court. "The Regional Court for Warsaw Praga-South hereby informs Mr. Marek Sznajderman of a hearing regarding usucaption. The case concerns a plot of land with an area of 1.5 hectares, division lot number..., Warsaw-Wawer district." And photographs. In the photographs there was a forest. And a piece of land between some suburban villas. Broken branches, a small clearing among pines and birches. The only traces of human activity were a well-trodden path leading to the railway tracks and small piles of brushwood.

You didn't know what it was about. No, you don't own any land there. Everything was sold after the war; it went into strangers' hands. And so, there's nothing left. What you'd like to say is: there was never anything there.

But in pre-war photographs this place is alive. A large, wooden, two-story house stands there. It's Villa Zacisze, also known as the Rozenberg Villa. On April 19, 1927, an advertisement was published in *Nasz Przęglad*: "Dr. I. Sznajderman, medical consultations on site at G. Rozenbergowa's boarding house in Miedzeszyn (privately owned, electricity). Quartz lamp, heat lamp, diathermy, electrotherapy, heliotherapy. Telephone: Podmiejski Radość 2." From then on, similar advertisements regularly appeared, until your mother Amelia took over management of the boarding house and started advertising it as "Dr. Sznajderman's boarding house in Miedzeszyn (Rosenberg Villa), formerly run by G. Rosenbergowa. Leave a message in person or phone Podmiejski Radość 2."

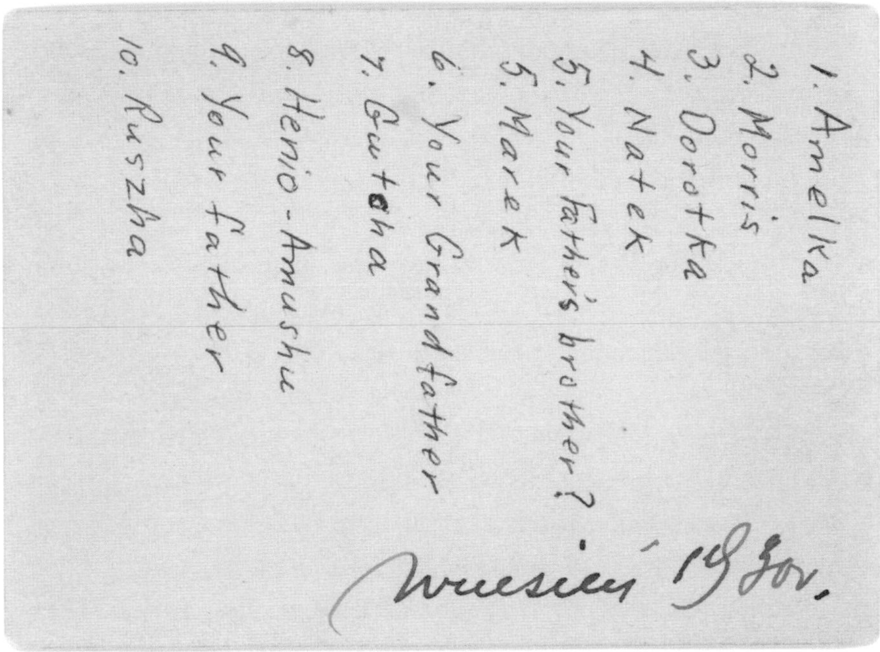
1. Amelka
2. Morris
3. Dorotka
4. Natek
5. Your father's brother?
5. Marek
6. Your Grandfather
7. Gutcha
8. Henio - Amushu
9. Your father
10. Ruszha

wrzesień 1930.

G. Rozenbergowa (the surname was spelled sometimes with an *s*, sometimes with a *z*) was your grandmother and my great-grandmother —Chana Gitla, née Weissbaum, who was called Gucia at home and Gustawa in Polish. Dr. I. Sznajderman was your father, Ignacy, a neurologist. In addition to the fee for a room, which ranged from four to six złoty per night, guests at the boarding house paid a municipal tax of twenty groszy and a hotel tax of thirty groszy daily, per person.

And so, the Rozenberg Villa is a comfortable house with electricity, offering modern medical treatments. It boasts a glassed-in veranda and a terrace for summertime relaxation and lounging. The veranda is spacious, with a pot containing a huge palm tree. The terrace is large, too; in photographs the entire family fits on it. The house has ornate latticework on the balconies and a light structure, typical of the middle-class wooden villas in the Warsaw suburbs at that time. Like most other villas of this style, it was probably erected from a simple pinewood frame. It stands in a forest glade where the sun shines through pine trees. And it will stay this way, it'll always seem like this to me: I only remember sunny days, although I know this is because Henryk, your uncle and the family photographer, only took out his camera when the sun was shining.

"Sculpted porches hidden among jasmine bushes and window shutters with stars cut into them, covered in Virginia creepers that were evenly pruned along the window frames to let in the light. Tiny balconies with latticework; turrets; pointed spires on the tiled roof, each decorated with a weathercock or a little flag-shaped weathervane. Glazed verandas, lounge areas with deck chairs—the height of fashion at the time. Airy, high-ceilinged rooms with large windows, full of sunlight, for both Christians and Jews with respiratory ailments. Summer and winter rooms, on the ground floor and upstairs, at affordable prices. The rooms upstairs were cheaper because of the climb, but they were cozier than the rooms below. Every possible comfort was guaranteed for patients and summertime vacationers—electricity, baths, showers, hot and cold water," writes Piotr Paziński in his book *The Boarding House*, which reconstructs that world.

I don't know, and neither do you, who built this house. It was probably constructed just after the First World War, perhaps in the early

1920s, by one of the many carpenters specializing in the architectural style invented by Michał Elwiro Andriolli. The wealthy and largely assimilated Rozenberg family was from Warsaw. I don't know exactly when or why Gustawa, née Weissbaum, and Selim Rozenberg decided to move to Miedzeszyn. Nor do I know why their house isn't mentioned in a brochure titled *Summer Resorts in Falenica* published in 1938. And yet the house existed, just as your grandparents and extended family existed (Grandpa Selim had an older brother named Józef and a sister named Salomea, and Grandma Gustawa had brothers, Jerzy and Maurycy, and a sister, Rózia), and your shy, introverted father was even a member of the inspection committee for the Friends of Miedzeszyn Association, which was founded in 1925 and had its headquarters on November 11th Street. The house existed and your mother, Amelia, liked to be photographed in front of it. This photograph from 1925 is captioned in her handwriting: "Behind me in the distance is our house. You wouldn't recognize it because the neighbor recently put up a fence. Miedzeszyn, July 1925." This photograph and these advertisements are the only tangible evidence. Without them, one might not believe any of it.

Because today there's no fence and no Amelia—known at home as Mata, born in Warsaw on January 15, 1904. She was full of life; in the photos she's always in whimsical poses wearing white or colorful dresses, sometimes even dressed up in costumes, with you and your younger brother Albert, whom everyone called Aluś. All the rest are gone, too: your grandfather Selim Rozenberg, his wife Chana Gitla, née Weissbaum (sometimes spelled Wajsbaum), and their sons, your uncles—Henryk the photographer and Natan, whom everyone called Natek.

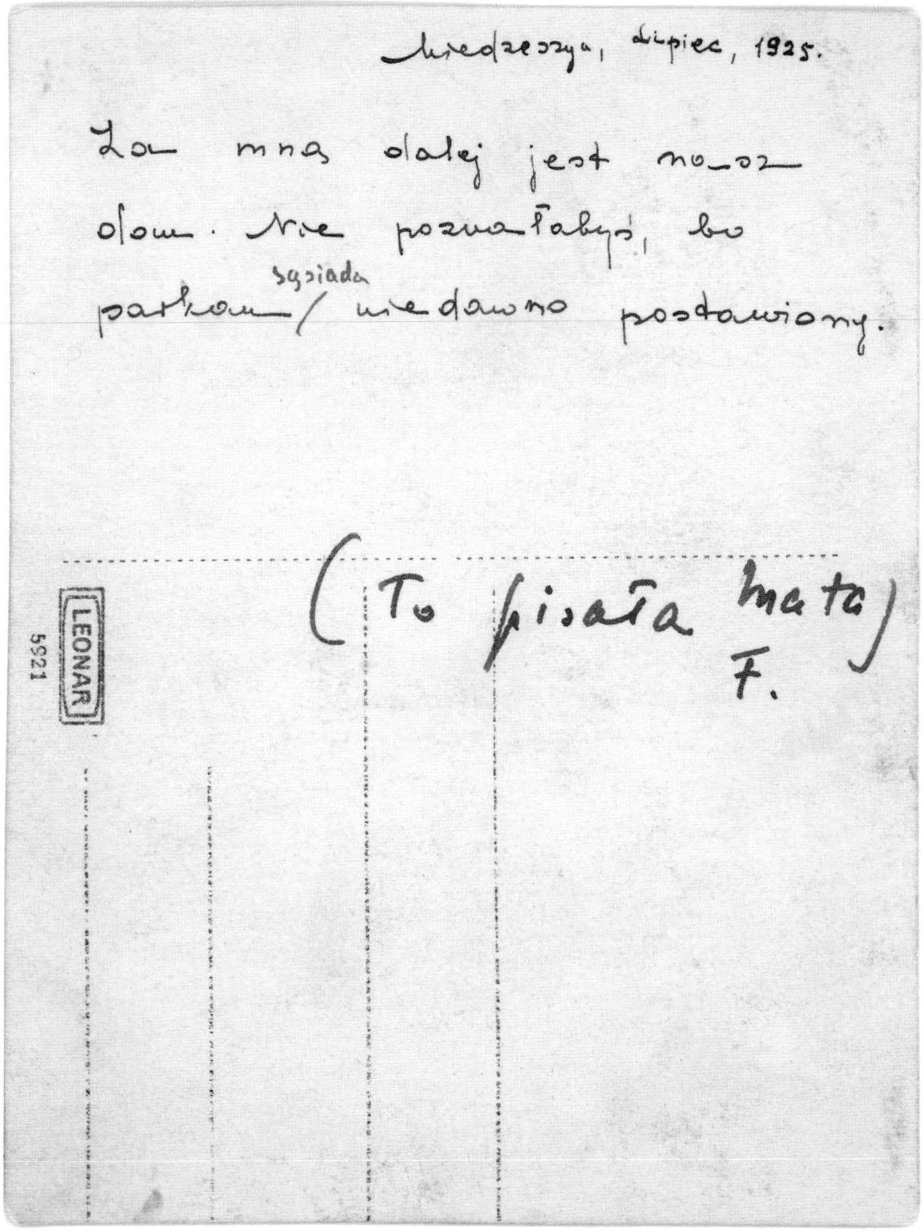
Miedzeszyn, lipiec, 1925.

Za mną dalej jest nasz dom. Nie poznałbyś, bo parkan (sąsiada) niedawno postawiony.

(To pisała Mata)
F.

LEONAR

5921

They've survived only in these photographs. Photographs that were miraculously saved, painstakingly preserved and sent to you from America just a few years ago. Together with some letters and that gray, linen, embroidered tablecloth that Amelia made for her favorite cousin before the war. The story of the fate of these photographs that survived the Holocaust overseas—Amelia liked to write and she liked her cousin, wanted to share her life story with her, so they survived, undamaged, and then, thanks to the surprising and miraculous efficiency of the American and Polish postal services, they found us and returned to you after more than seventy years—is a symbolic story about life in the pre-Holocaust world. At the opposite extreme of these, with their inviolability, their undisturbed state, are the very few photos taken later, during the Holocaust, that survived—photos, as Jacek Leociak writes, that are "damaged, torn, darkened, corroded," which experienced something liminal and inexpressible, and by their very appearance testify to the Holocaust. Looked at today from the perspective of hindsight, they become tangible evidence of the Holocaust—something, as Susan Sontag says, "directly stenciled off the real, like a footprint or a death mask." The voice of these damaged photos is, to quote Leociak again, "muted, obliterated and anguished, often barely audible or discernible," speaking to us in a way that is "broken and fragmentary." For these photos, in their damaged and mutilated state, express the impossibility of representing that reality. "Nothing resembles what happened there at that time, and so distortion is the only possible form of representation. [...] Distortion which in itself reveals the touch of that reality."

The photographs from Miedzeszyn speak in a different voice: strong and joyful. Neither the Holocaust nor the passage of time have disturbed their physical substance. In these photographs, your childhood world is bright, sunny, and pleasant. You're surrounded by a large, happy, multi-generational family. You're embracing each other, fooling around, laughing. There's so much warmth and love between all of you. Would it be easier for me if there weren't? Here you are sitting on Grandpa Selim's shoulders with some bushes, perhaps sumac, behind you (it's August 1930, you're three years old), and here—on January 3, 1928—you're posing for a photograph on the veranda in a huge, white cap while Amelia embraces you. In the summer of 1936, you're sitting on a bench in Śródborów—Amelia in the middle, with you and Aluś cuddled up to her on either side. Amelia is wearing a floral-patterned dress; you're holding a scooter and Aluś is petting a kitten. A child's spade lies abandoned under the bench. You and Aluś are wearing identical striped shirts, and on your bare, suntanned feet you have identical marks left by your sandals. I can't tear my eyes away from these marks. They're like the very essence of transience, emphasizing even more strongly the ephemerality of this long-lost moment. The moment is lost, but at the same time it's preserved forever within this sensitive frame. This is precisely where the miracle of photography lies.

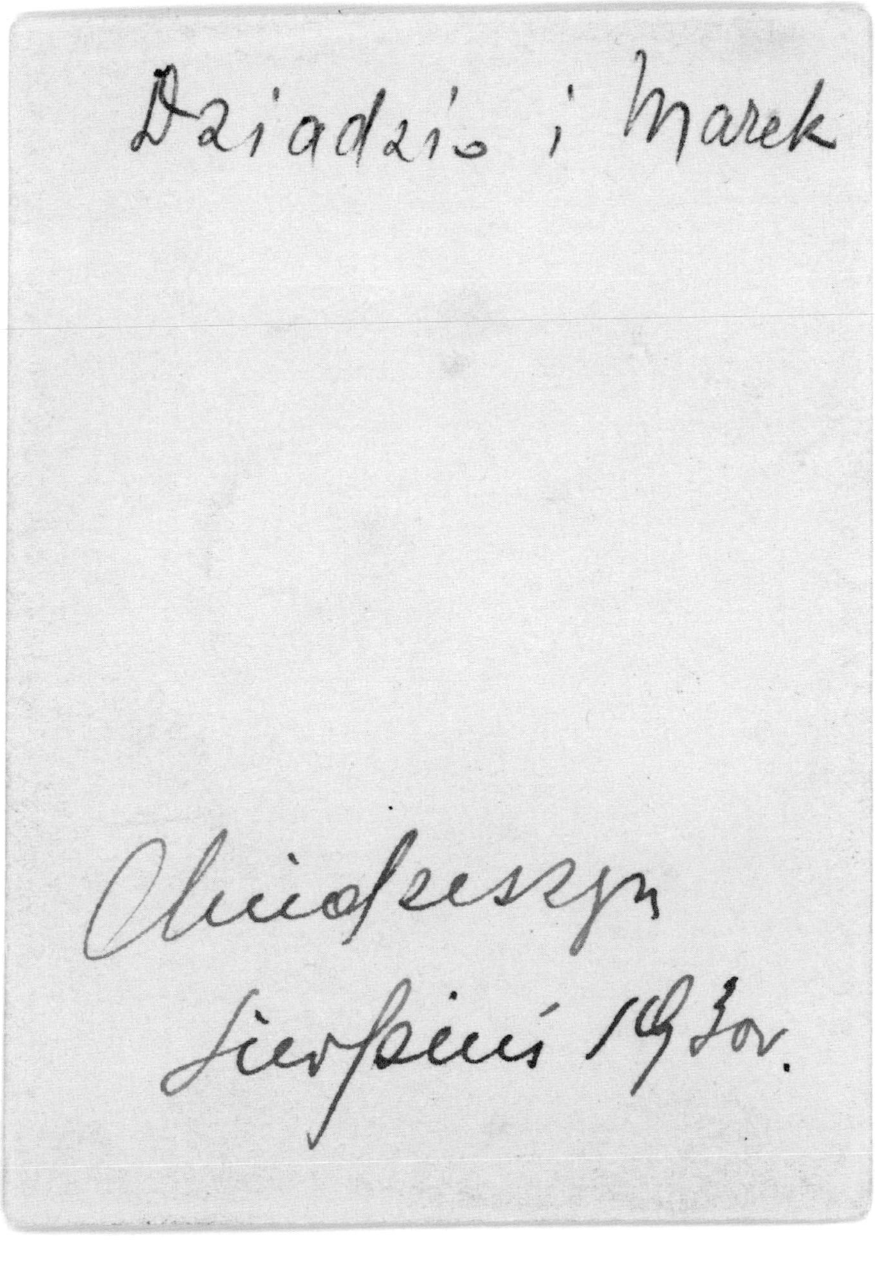

Dziadzio i Marek

Chodorszyn

Sierpień 1930r.

3. I. 28.

Na werandzie.

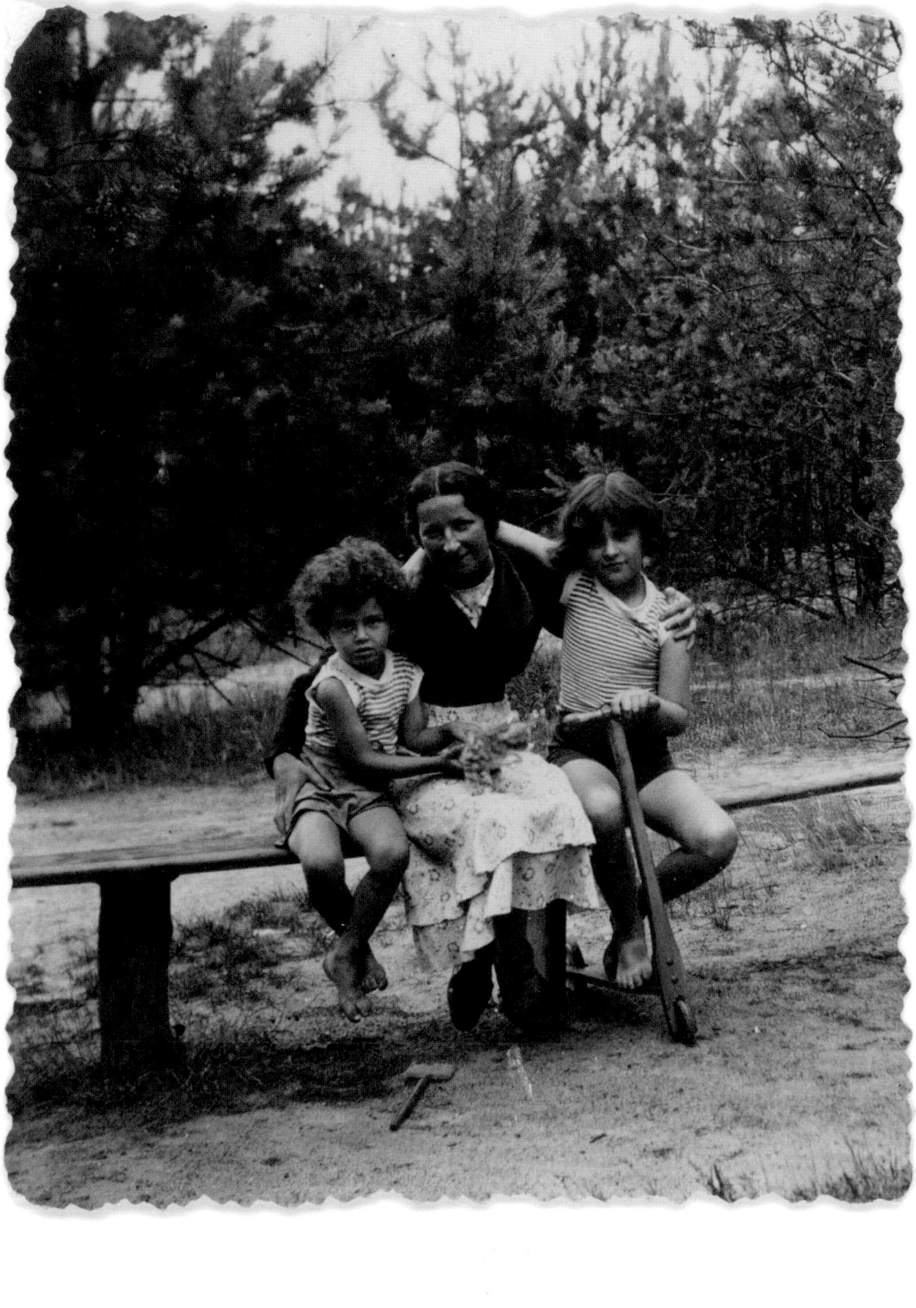

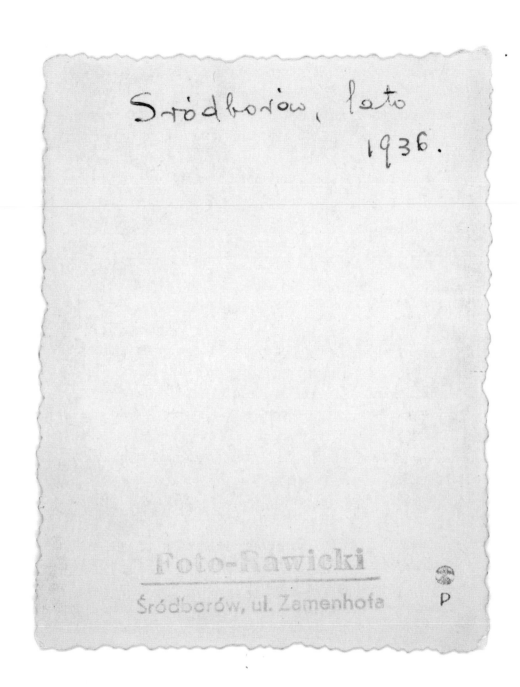

Śródborów, lato
1936.

Foto-Rawicki

Śródborów, ul. Zemenhofa

I can also picture you sitting together like this, with you on one side of your mother and Aluś on the other, snuggled closely to her on the hard seats of the commuter train of the Vistula River Railway. You board the train at Warsaw's main railway station ("electric traction, trains every 15–20 minutes in summer, third-class ticket price—80 groszy") or at the station in Gdańsk—close to the place from which, a few years later, your father and brother will travel to their deaths. But it's not time for that yet. Because now Aluś, cuddled up close to your mother, is traveling on a sunny summer day not to Treblinka, but to Miedzeszyn, and your father is waiting for you on the platform. I'm sure you also traveled sometimes by "choo-choo"—the narrow-gauge train from the Kierbedź Bridge station in Warsaw ("every half hour in summer, third-class ticket price—80 groszy"). In reality, it's possible you lounged comfortably on soft pillows in first or second class, not holding drab little cardboard tickets but rather those green or blue ones. But in my imagination—I don't know where these images come from—you're traveling in third class, squeezed together on a wooden seat. You ate sweet yeast buns on the train. You hired a horse-drawn carriage from the station.

Sometimes, I imagine, Natan would give you a ride from Warsaw in his new car. You would cross the Vistula River on the Poniatowski Bridge and then drive along the rocky Grochowska gorge to Wawer and Zastów. From Wawer onward it was just a dirt road. Or you might have taken the Miedzeszyńska highway along the banks of the Vistula River and through Zbytki. That road was paved.

Then I see you going together to buy fresh vegetables at the market on Sosnowa Street. Or to the post office on November 11th

Street to send some postcards. When you needed toiletries or household supplies you stopped by Tadeusz Sikorski's Perfumery and Hygienic Supplies Shop next to the post office. I see you strolling through fragrant pine forests and sandy birch groves. And kicking a ball around in sunny meadows. Near Falenica you pass Jews engrossed in holy books, with little groups of traditionally dressed children playing around them. Goats graze between the houses; their milk is good for consumptives and nursing mothers. "Goats nibbled at acacia bushes, tore the green bark right down to the white wood beneath, and kicked sand out from under the moss. This area was always very dry," recalls Bogdan Wojdowski, another frequent visitor to the boarding houses along the railway line, in his book *Tamta strona* (Over there). Sometimes on warm days you swam in the Vistula River. It was only one and a half kilometers from your house. But you had to watch out for dangerous eddies. For larger purchases, you drove to Handlowa Street in Falenica, which had recently been paved. And surely the peddlers from Otwock and Karczew (both Jewish and non-Jewish) who stopped by other summer resorts along the railway line would come with heavy baskets to your house, too, "bringing chickens and fruit of various kinds, calling out their wares as they approached." A mobile hairdresser would appear, an ice-vendor with vanilla ice cream, and a confectioner from as far away as Otwock with boxes full of shortbread, all of them followed from villa to villa by a colorful, noisy throng of beggars.

I'm curious to know what your relations with your Polish neighbors were like. Did you have any contact with them at all? I doubt it. Polish people didn't tend to socialize with assimilated Jewish families, but if you did know them, I would really like to believe that it wasn't your friends or neighbors who came rushing in horse-drawn carts to loot houses in Otwock, Falenica, and Miedzeszyn after the liquidation of the ghettos there in 1942. That it wasn't your friends or neighbors who broke windows and doors, who stole clothing, tableware, linen, and furniture. Somewhere, I no longer remember where, I came across a description of Polish looters running through the deserted streets of small towns along the Otwock railway line wearing stolen Jewish clothing: fur caps, black hats, long cloaks, and dark dresses. I hope this "enraged beast in human form" which, "having caught the still-fresh scent of blood, prowled like jackals and hyenas among the cooling corpses," as the evidently shocked author of a news bulletin titled *News from Otwock*, published on September 18, 1942, describes the Polish looters, were not the same people with whom you used to exchange pleasantries while strolling along the streets of Falenica, or with whom you played volleyball in the nearby glades. Or with whom you chatted while standing in line at the post office, or whom Ignacy treated at his medical clinic.

The mobs of looters, according to the newspaper *Nowy Dzień* in its issue published on August 27, 1942, even included members of the intelligentsia.

But by that time, you, Aluś, and Amelia were no longer there. Neither was your father, Ignacy, who'd worked as a doctor at the Zofiówka Sanatorium in Otwock. He didn't witness the massacre of his mentally ill patients in 1942, which was described in the following words by Zalman Goldin in his testimony submitted to the Jewish Historical Institute: "They were herded along, wearing their long hospital gowns. As they went, they held up the hems of their gowns to make it easier to walk. On the way to their slaughter, they shouted odd, random phrases, such as 'little green pigeons on heads,' 'where's grandma,' 'we're having a terrible heatwave,' etc. Some of them escaped, some were killed. Some of them ran away, some were forced to dig graves. Some dashed at the Germans and beat them. One smashed a German's head with a shovel. Three hundred Jews—invalids—were killed. While digging the graves they sprinkled sand over themselves, lay on the ground and refused to dig, and clung to the Germans' necks. The invalids continued their odd behavior while the Germans killed them one by one."

But that will all come later.

For now, I have two photographs in front of me that were taken at the clinic just after you were born. You're lying peacefully in swaddling clothes and your eyes are closed. There are little bottles and vials in the cupboard and on the table next to Amelia. She wrote on the back of this photo that it was taken by Natck, who came to the hospital with his camera.

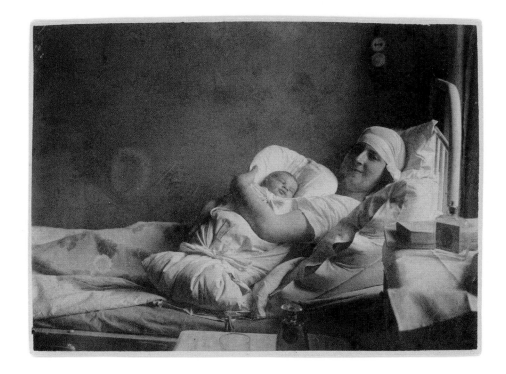

You were born during the night between Sunday and Monday. Fortunately, it wasn't hot—the daytime temperature ranged from ten to seventeen degrees. "Quite pleasant weather overall, with an overcast sky that is rapidly clearing up." A good day to give birth.

At that time, Warsaw covered an area of 12,000 hectares and was sparsely populated; there were 22.25 square meters per capita. The press reported that no major outbreak of scarlet fever was expected that year, which must have pleased Amelia because twenty-five cases had been recorded in August, just before you were born, as well as thirty-one cases of typhoid, two of diphtheria, seventy-two of measles, twenty of rubella, thirteen of whooping cough, fourteen of dysentery, and one hundred twenty of tuberculosis. The Ministry of Foreign Affairs denied reports circulated by the American Consulate that cholera was rampant in Poland. In the first half of August, ninety-two Jewish people died in the capital city. Intensive measures were being implemented to improve standards of hygiene. There was an ongoing battle against extortionate housing prices. The butchers' association announced a decrease in the wholesale price of beef by twenty or even thirty groszy per kilogram. There were plans to lay eight kilometers of new tram tracks: for example, the tram line from Leszno Street to Gorczewska Street would be extended by five kilometers, right to the border of Greater Warsaw, and the tracks running along Młynarska Street to the Evangelical cemetery would be extended by one kilometer, as well as the tracks through the Targówek district to the viaduct and the Bródno cemetery. There was a newly opened school in Śródborów for children aged six to fourteen, run by Julia Wilczyńska, called the House in the Forest. "What wonderful and rapid results there are at the free school in the countryside," wrote Janusz Korczak, "where nobody demands impossible things from the children, where the children are not impeded or restrained, and where their strengths are unleashed... Parents beg for such schools..." The House in the Forest was modelled on schools such as the Landerziehungsheim (an institute promoting the rational education of children in a rural setting). Children from poor tenement houses in the center of Warsaw could rapidly improve their health and spiritual equilibrium in the dry, healthy climate of Śródborów, within a friendly, supportive environment.

On the back of a photograph taken two days later, on August 31, Amelia wrote: "At the clinic. My face is obscured by a flower—it looks like a mask." Yes, the elements of masquerade inherent in everyday life were essential for my grandmother's happiness. The little bottles and vials have been replaced by flowers, lots of flowers. A croissant lies on a small, white plate on the bedside table next to a white teacup, a watch, and a newspaper. Your eyes are open now.

From another photograph, dated October 18, I learn that Amelia posed with you (less than two months old) in her arms for Maksymilian (Maks) Eljowicz, a well-known Jewish artist from Warsaw. During the war, Eljowicz, a painter, graphic designer, and interior decorator from a poor Hasidic family from Raciąż, near Płock, would paint portraits of German officers in the Warsaw ghetto. On August 25, 1942, at the age of fifty-two, he would be transported to Treblinka. But that will happen later. For now, Maksymilian Eljowicz is painting. He's wearing a long doctor's coat over his elegant suit and is gazing attentively at his model. All these different realities, these lost worlds of mine, accumulate within this photograph and pile up: there's the portrait in it—the only trace of this painting by Eljowicz—but also the very act of painting. There's an artist at work and a mother holding her child. The following words are written on the back of the photograph in Amelia's hand-writing: "Posing. As a reward for my efforts, Eljowicz will give me the portrait (he'll also have a copy—he'll paint two)."

You recall that portraits of Amelia were also painted by the famous artist and typographer Henryk Berlewi. They didn't even survive in photographs.

In a photo taken in September 1930, you're already three years old, and you're leaning against your grandmother Gucia's knees in the glassed-in veranda. Other family members are standing next to you under the large potted palm tree: Amelia, elegant as always in a white dress and necklace; Amelia's uncle Maurycy, who's visiting from America and goes by the English version of his name, Morris; his wife Dorotka; your uncle Natan; and your grandfather Selim. The men are wearing ties. The veranda is flooded with sunlight.

In another photo taken on the same day, Selim is reading the September 3 issue of *Nasz Przegląd*, Natek is standing behind him, and Dorotka is reading the newspaper over his shoulder. Morris, your grandmother Gucia, and Amelia are examining something in another newspaper spread out on a large table covered with a white oilcloth. It was probably at this table that the boarding house's guests ate their meals, while the sunshine reflected off their plates.

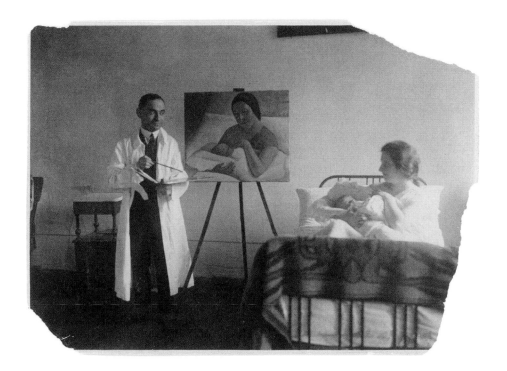

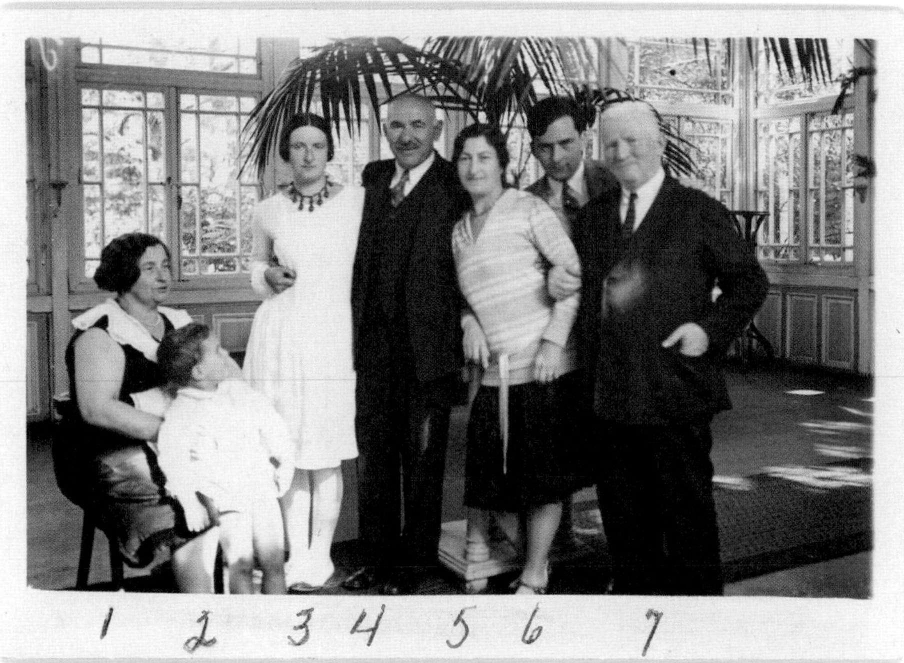
1 2 3 4 5 6 7

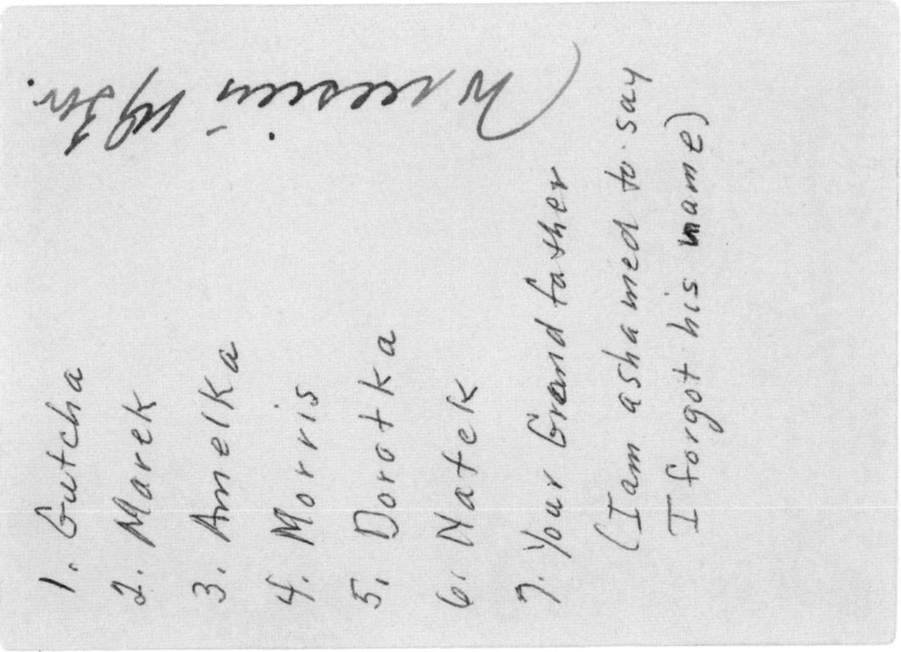
1. Gutcha
2. Marek
3. Amelka
4. Morris
5. Dorotka
6. Natek
7. Your Grandfather
(I am ashamed to say
I forgot his name)

1 2　　　3　4　5　　6

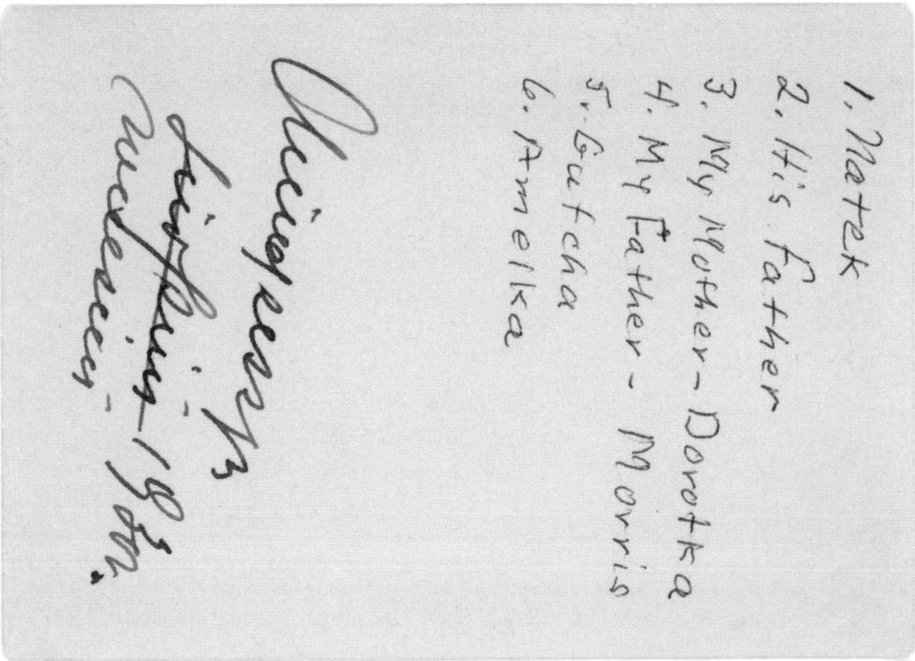

1. Matek
2. His father
3. My Mother—Dorotka
4. My Father—Morris
5. Gufcha
6. Amelka

Ciechocinek
Sierpnia 1931
Wakacye

What did your grandfather find interesting in the newspaper he was reading? I inspect it carefully, trying to imagine this scene. It's my way of conjuring them into life and entering their world—the only way I have. Was he reading about the accident at the corner of Krakowskie Przedmieście Avenue and Miodowa Street, when a small truck speeding from the direction of the Kierbedź Bridge crashed into the traffic island by the tram stop? You lived close to this spot, in an apartment in the building at 58 Krakowskie Przedmieście Avenue. You often crossed paths in the front entrance with the writer Boy-Żeleński and his wife Zofia Pareńska, known to her friends as Fusia, and on Saturdays you rubbed shoulders with their many distinguished guests. I can almost hear Selim saying to your mother: "It happened near your place, Mata." Or was he looking through the ads, comparing the prices at rival boarding houses? Did he notice that Justyna Elbaum still had rooms available nearby in Miedzeszyn, with gourmet kosher cuisine, electricity, and "significantly reduced prices"? And that "Goldberg's boarding house in Mr. Szuldiner's Villa," with kosher cuisine, was also trying to attract guests with low prices? For I doubt that Selim was interested in buying "a coypu fur coat for men, Franciszkańska Street 30–95, 4–7 p.m."

That day you also took several photos on the bench in front of your house and in a meadow. In one of them, Amelia, still in her white dress and wearing white tennis shoes, is embracing Morris. Morris is holding his hat and sunglasses in his left hand. They're standing among tall pine trees, with the intricate latticework of the boarding house's balconies in the background. I like this photograph very much. There's warmth and tenderness in it, and Amelia's white dress and shoes contrast beautifully with Morris's dark clothing. There are some details here, finally: a hat and sunglasses, and the ornately decorated balconies. And this is why, even though what's important here is memory and life, not art, this photograph so beautifully evokes the words of Susan Sontag: "Time eventually positions most photographs, even the most amateurish, at the level of art."

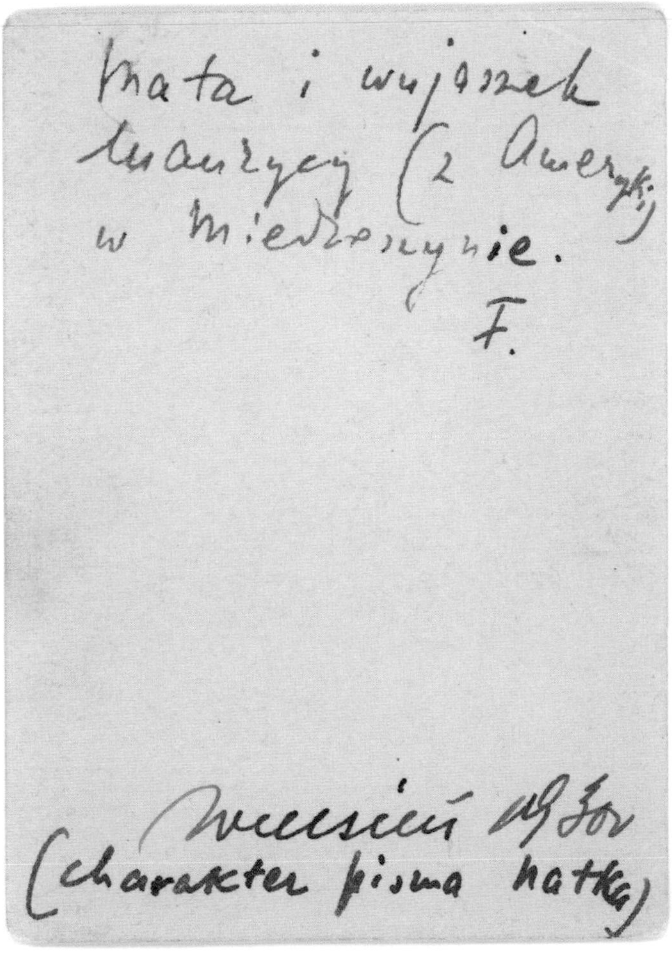

mata i wujaszek
Maurycy (z Ameryki)
w Miedzeszynie.
F.

wrzesień 1930r
(charakter pisma matki)

164

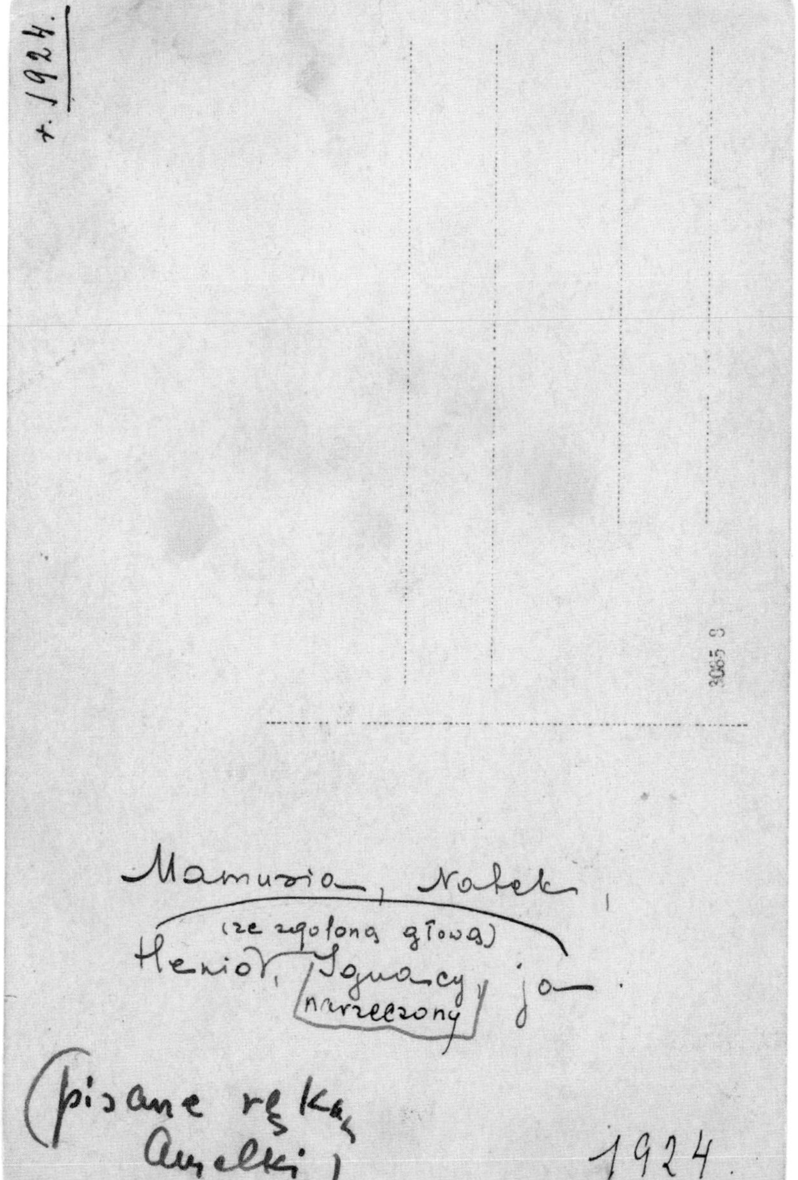
r. 1924.
Mamusia, Natek,
(ze zgoloną głową)
Henio, Ignacy, ja.
narzeczony
(pisane ręką
Anielki)
1924.

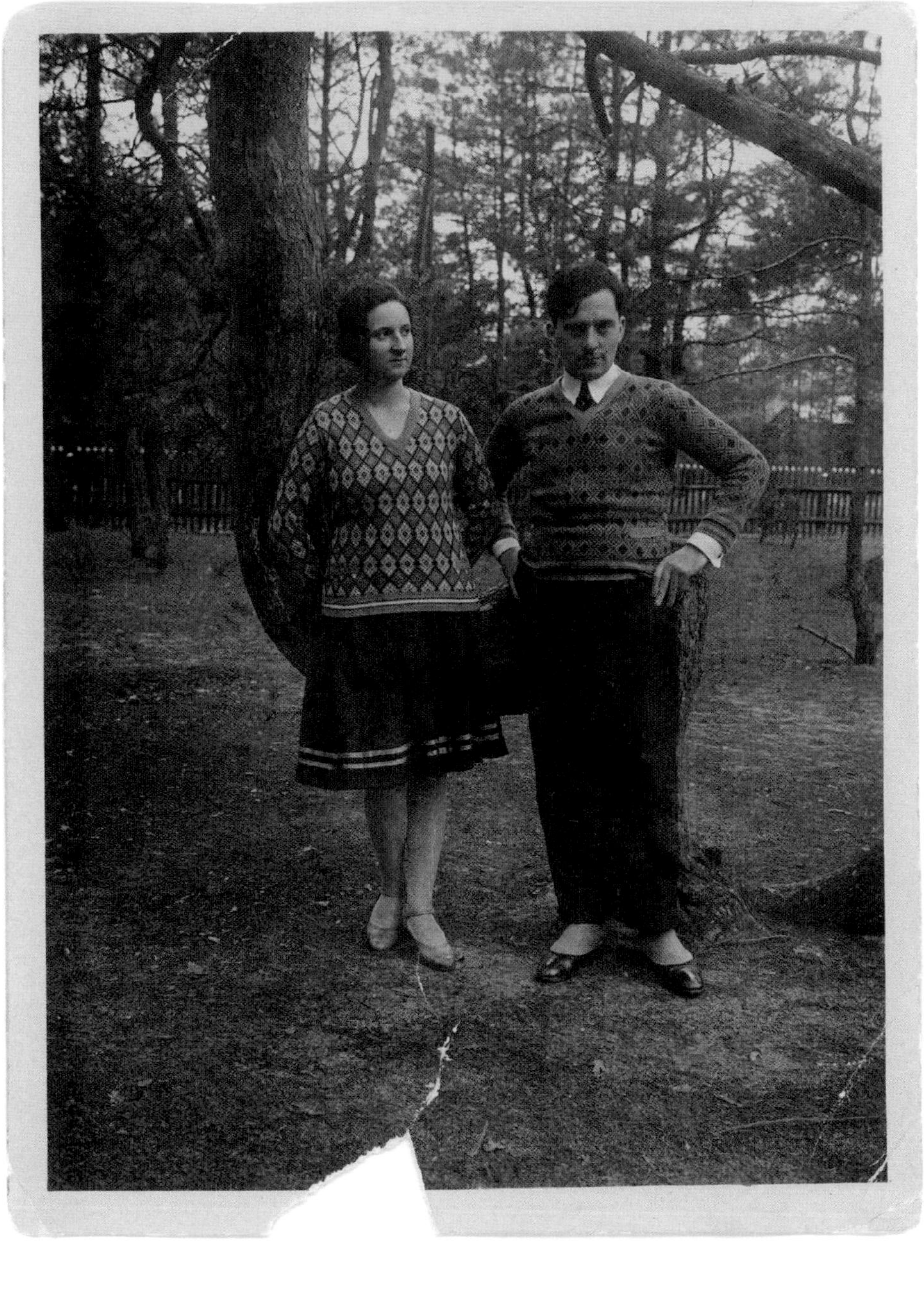

5.XI.27.

i hatek

1 2 3 5 6 8 10
      4   7 9 11

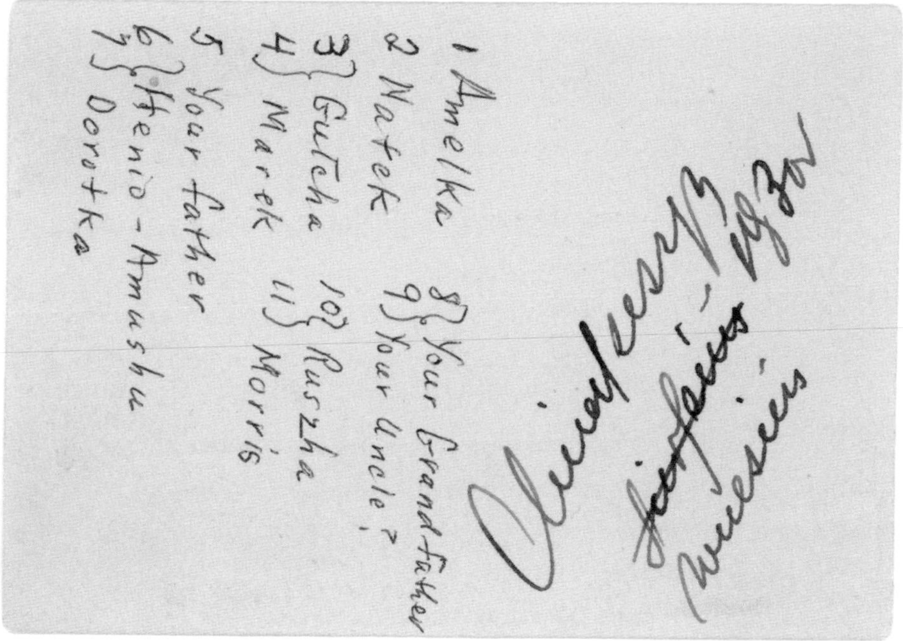
1 Amelka
2 Natek
3} Gutcha
4} Marek
5 Your father
6} Henio - Amushu
7} Dorotka
8} Your Grandfather
9} Your Uncle ?
10} Ruszka
11} Morris

Now let's go back in time a few years. It's 1924 and you haven't entered the world yet. Natek, Amelia, and Ignacy (Amelia's fiancé) are standing in a row, and Henryk is kneeling with his hair cut very short (he put a handkerchief under his left knee so as not to soil his trousers). Gucia, who will become your grandmother in three years' time, is sitting with her hands in her lap, smiling serenely. I don't know who took this photo. It's certainly posed: Natan and Henryk are wearing identical bow ties, white shirts, and trousers, and Amelia is dressed as whimsically and elegantly as ever, with a white headscarf. It's clear they liked to have fun and dress up. Amelia and Natek also dressed up for a photograph taken on November 5, 1927: they're both wearing colorful V-neck sweaters with geometric patterns. Amelia is casting a sidelong glance at her brother.

I memorize their faces and figures, I collect details and objects, I catalog their clothes and fancy outfits, I catch moments and observe feelings, I look carefully at a spot left by the sun, I collect little bits of the life that has vanished without a trace. For nothing else remains for me of any of them. Only Gucia's tender gaze at her grandson, not quite two months old, as she holds him in her arms. And Amelia's sense of humor when she wrote on the back of a photo of you in swaddling clothes, lying on two bentwood chairs under a clothesline where diapers are hanging to dry, taken on November 3, 1927: "Little Marek in his atelier." Your eyes are wide open, gazing at the sky or perhaps the treetops.

Photography, to quote Susan Sontag again, provides me with material evidence, enabling me to believe they existed.

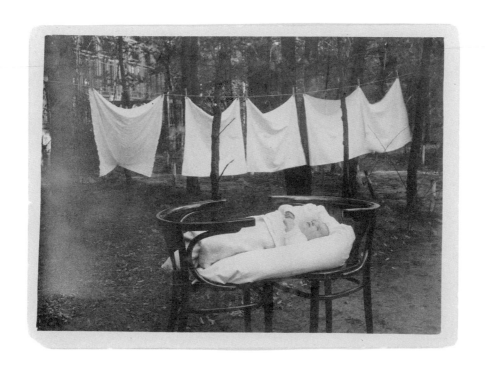

A photo taken on August 15, 1930, also provides such material evidence. Was this when your uncle Natan bought his car (a Hanomag 2/10 PS Kommissbrot, 1925–28)? He took a photo of himself in it with you on his lap, nearly three years old, parked in a field in Miedzeszyn. Natan is smoking a cigarette. The car's registration number is SL 10528: the letters on the license plate seem to indicate that Natan bought the car in Silesia, while the numbers suggest Poznań.

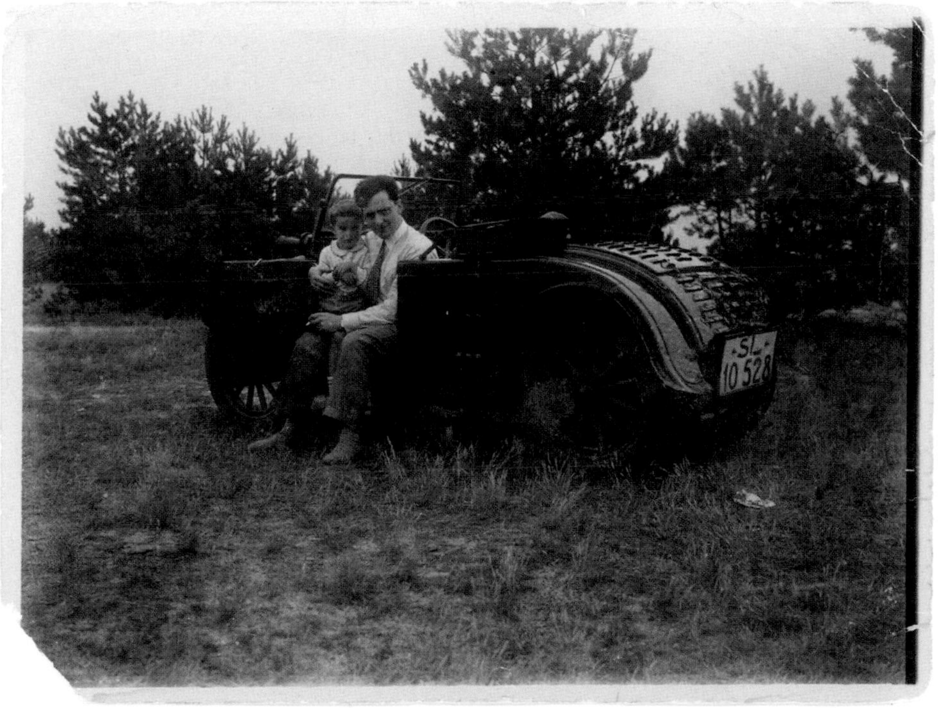
SL
10 528

Marek rysuje.   JM.

Rano przyszedł do nas Marek na
werandę i zaczął próbować moje kolorowe
ołówki. Złapałem go na migawkę, gdy
wcale nie wiedział, że go fotografuję.
te białe plama na nosie to zakończenie
ołówka.

                    (To pisał Henio Majzner
                                        f.

MIEDZESZYN   12.X.1932.

Further material evidence is a photo with "Marek drawing" written on the back of it, with an added note: "In the morning Marek came to us on the veranda and started trying out my colored pencils. I took a snapshot of him while he was completely unaware. The white spot on his nose is the tip of a pencil." Thanks to these words and this photograph, we know that on October 12, 1932, you were drawing with colored pencils, with great concentration, on the veranda in Miedzeszyn. We know what kind of pajamas you were wearing. We also know how the last rays of October sunlight were falling. The day was rather overcast, with some sunny spells. You are now five years old. There are seven more years of happy childhood ahead of you. This is why I'm so moved by a photograph taken in Warsaw just before the war—on June 5, 1939. You're saying goodbye to relatives who are leaving for the US. The adults are sitting on a sofa in a dark room with floral wallpaper behind them. Aluś, your brother, is on the floor, and you're on the left-hand side at a table covered with a tablecloth. You have a keen gaze and a watch on your left wrist. In an issue of *Mały Przegląd* dated January 27, 1939, I discovered an announcement that you had correctly answered all the questions in the 13th Recreational Tournament organized by the magazine. Everyone is cheerful, smiling. And yet this photo, although so joyful, fills me with sadness and dread because I know more than you do, even though you're the ones who were there, not I.

J.M.
Warszawa
5.VI.1939.

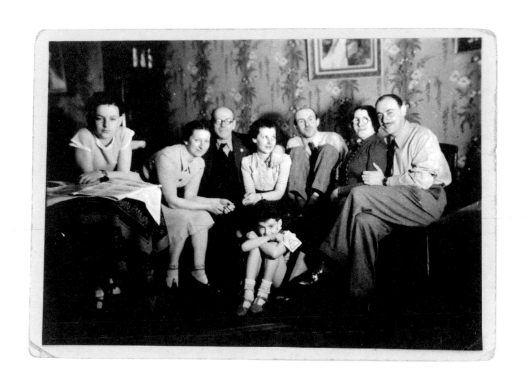

Yes, all of these photographs survived the war physically intact, unscathed by the Holocaust. They were expertly developed and the sodium thiosulphate was rinsed off very well, for which there was neither time nor space during the war. This is why there are brown spots, rust-colored stains, smudges, and shadows in most of the photos taken during the Holocaust. And yet, even in these seemingly perfect photos a shadow appears, although it's not a literal, material shadow. It's the shadow of the approaching times, because we know more than you do. We know how it ends. Therefore, these too are stained with death. In fact, every photograph, even the most joyful one, speaks "of death in the future tense," to quote Jacek Leociak once again. Especially when it was taken just before the war—then the shadow becomes darker and thicker. Like in this photograph, seemingly the most cheerful one—you and Aluś are dressed in light shirts (yours is checkered and Aluś's is striped), looking so alike, gazing straight ahead and smiling. It's hard for me to find the words to describe your smiles. It's the year 1937.

Two years later, on August 27, 1939, you turned twelve. It was overcast and there was a light drizzle. The temperature fluctuated between thirteen and twenty degrees. In the afternoon the weather improved, and the sun even came out. But the chill and the rain had discouraged the summer tourists, and they began heading back to Warsaw earlier than usual. Wagons and covered carts laden with washtubs, clothing, bedding, pots, deck chairs, and Primus stoves slowly wound their way toward the capital city. Soon the road was to be significantly improved—construction work was already in progress on a six-kilometer stretch of the Warsaw–Otwock highway from the boundaries of Greater Warsaw to Miedzeszyn, along the Miedzeszyński Embankment. The roadwork was scheduled to last until 1942.

Activity also increased on the regional bus lines. Because of the interest in returning home early from holidays in the summer of 1939, "many extra vehicles were added on weekdays, and on weekends when necessary," on routes such as Warsaw–Świder–Otwock–Śródborów.

Leaders of the Jewish community urged people returning from their holidays to take an active part in digging anti-aircraft trenches in response to an appeal from the mayor of Warsaw.

On the first of September you were supposed to start a new school; you had finished the primary school on Miodowa Street (you remember reading books in the street while walking to school—your favorite was *Arsène Lupin, Gentleman Burglar*), and even though you were sick with whooping cough at the time, you were the only Jew to be admitted to the Tadeusz Czacki State High School. But you're not thinking about that yet. You're thinking about your birthday, instead—the last birthday you'll spend with your family, the last birthday of your childhood. You don't yet know that very soon you'll be forced to become an adult. And that you'll be utterly alone.

"The beautiful dream that we unfold and extend…

Monchoachi

Translated from French by Eric Fishman

Photographs by David Damoison

The beautiful dream that we unfold and extend,
ruined, in the course of a sublime mockery;
beauty defeated by the measure of a sobering glance,
reflected from a bitterly earned truth.

You, aubain, you trace, cross the unlivable place,
distraught, crack it, move it,
lift it up high, spin like a water wheel.
And your goods can be taken away.

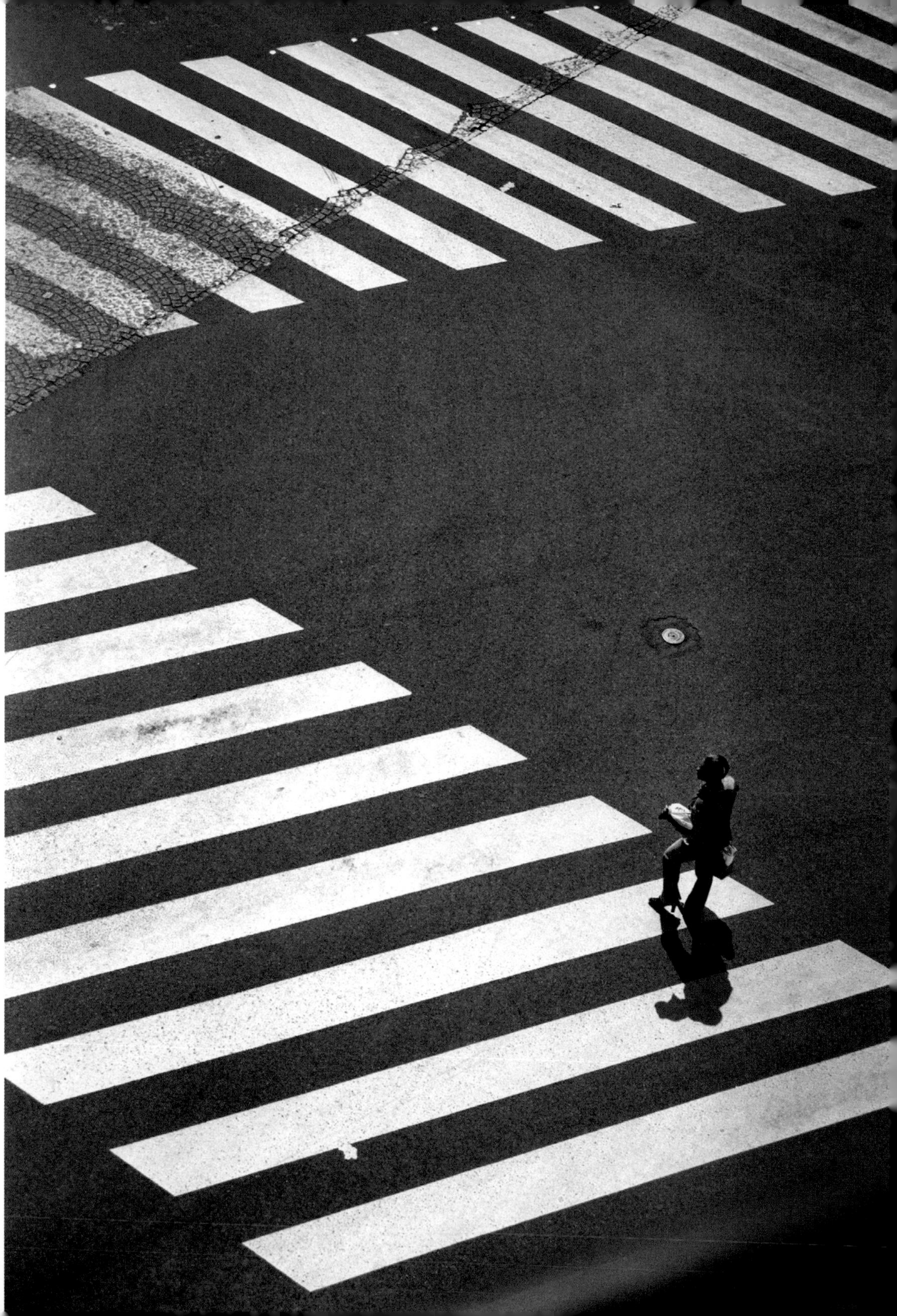

Between letter and body, an analogy exists
more than an allegory, an identical signifier:
one like the other signifies presence.
And when the body and writing show themselves
(on dull walls, along dreary
corridors) they don't speak only of their own
instability, the bitter solitude that slips
from an exhausted glance, they speak of the instability
that belongs to presence in and of itself.

Between letter and body, there's another
analogy that raises this one to an identical
destiny: shunted, transferred, moved
from one word to another word, from one place to another
place, one like the other is conceived only
when the pieces are brought together: as the letter begins
to sing, as the body is set abuzz.

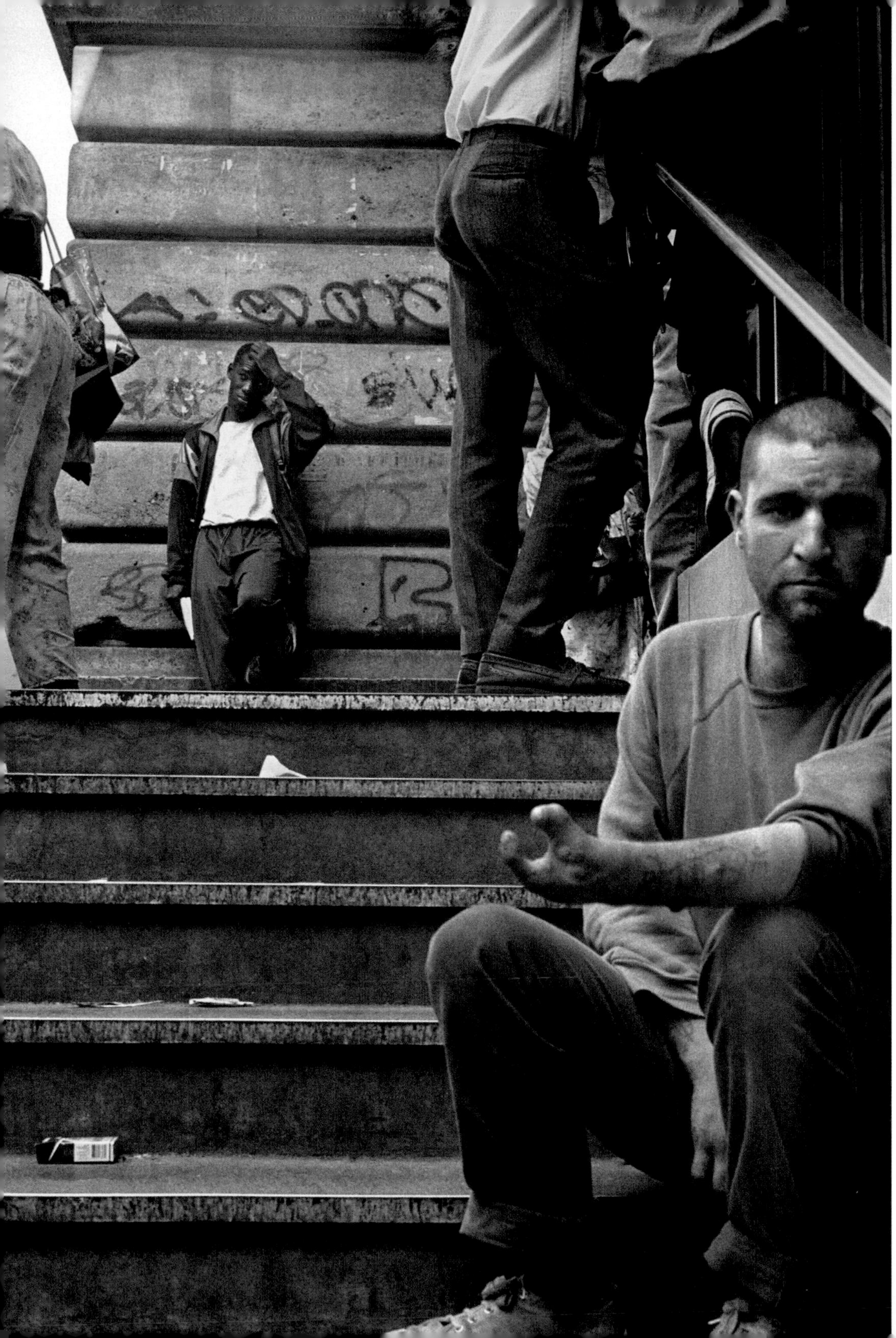

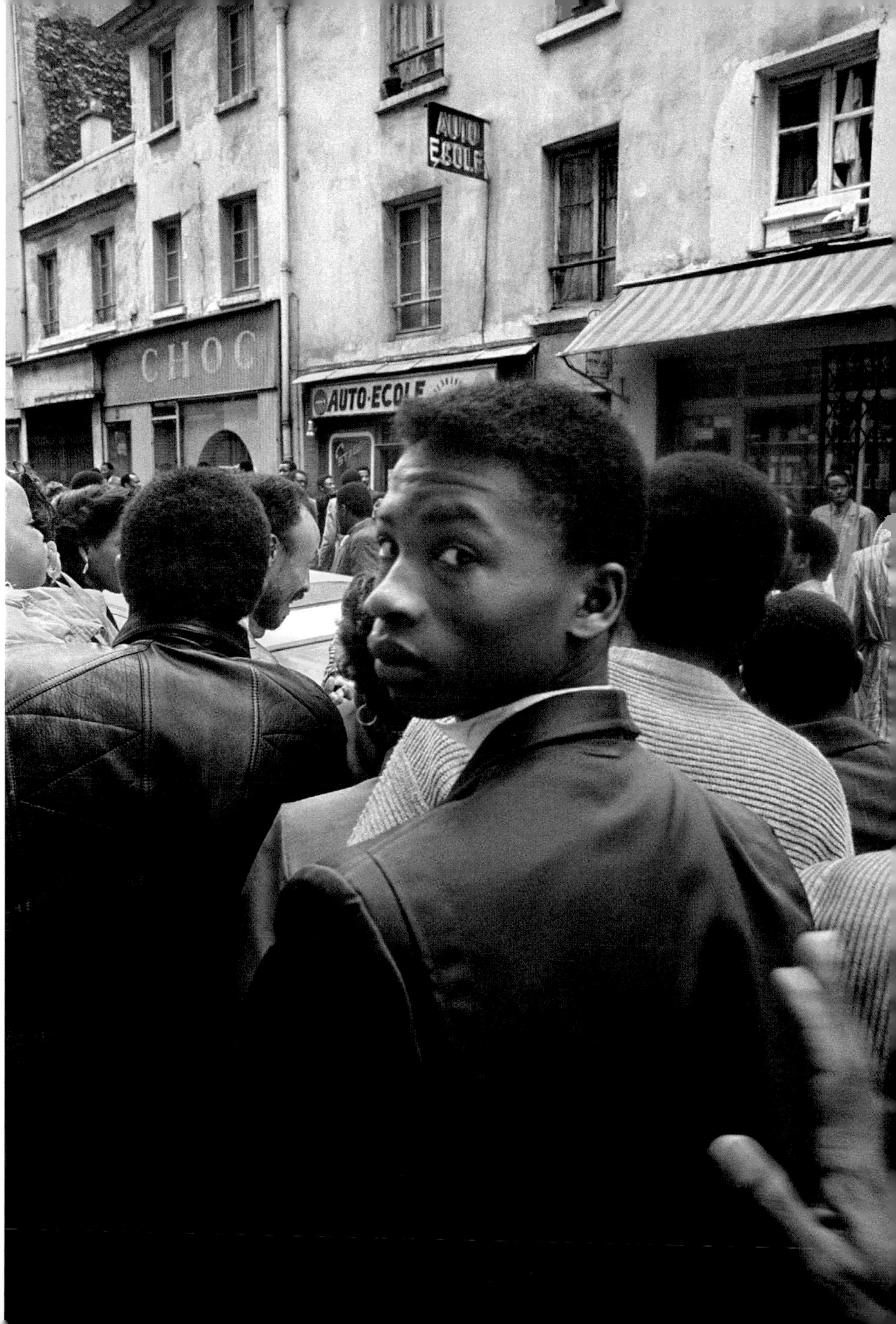

AUTO
ECOLE
CHOC
AUTO·ECOLE

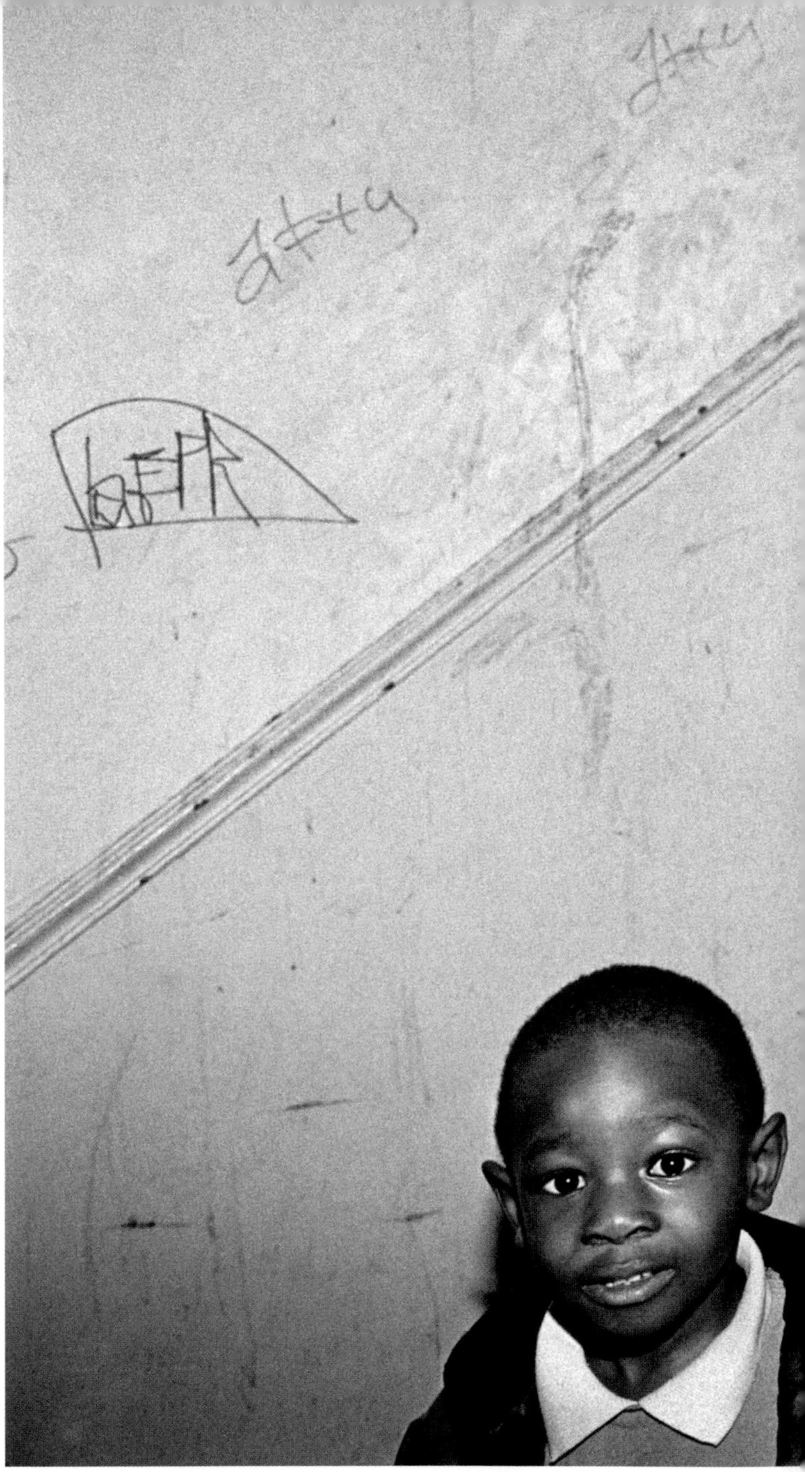

Ripped body, ripped letter, letter that grips,
trashed body, torn, trampled, body split
you're tripping, spell an alph'bet
yelled names, called bodies
rung by rung, step by step,
bodies you stain, you step,
you screen under letters you shell,
you spell, body we grip, rap, trap,
trip, ha! Sick. Check it out: go on.

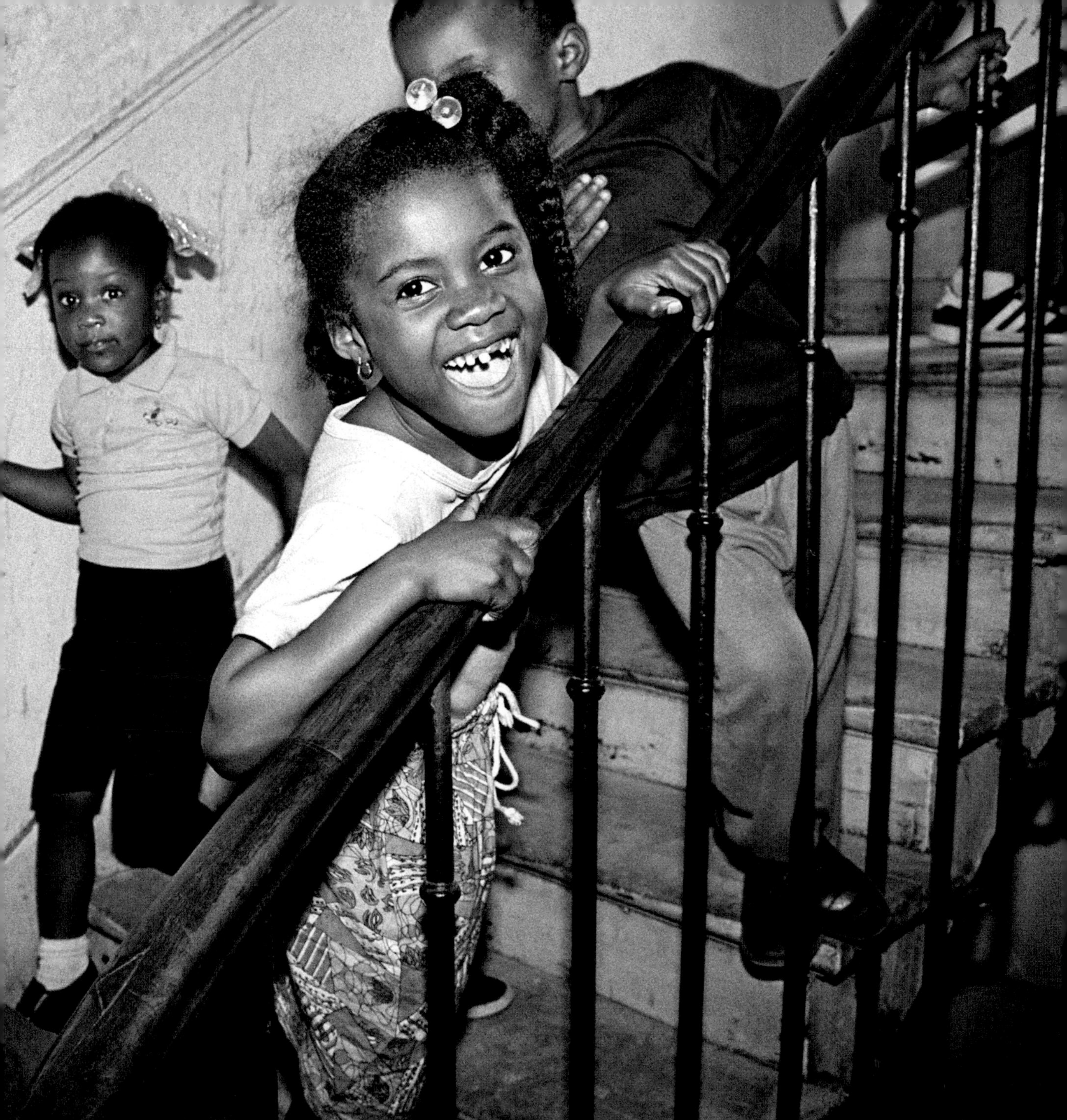

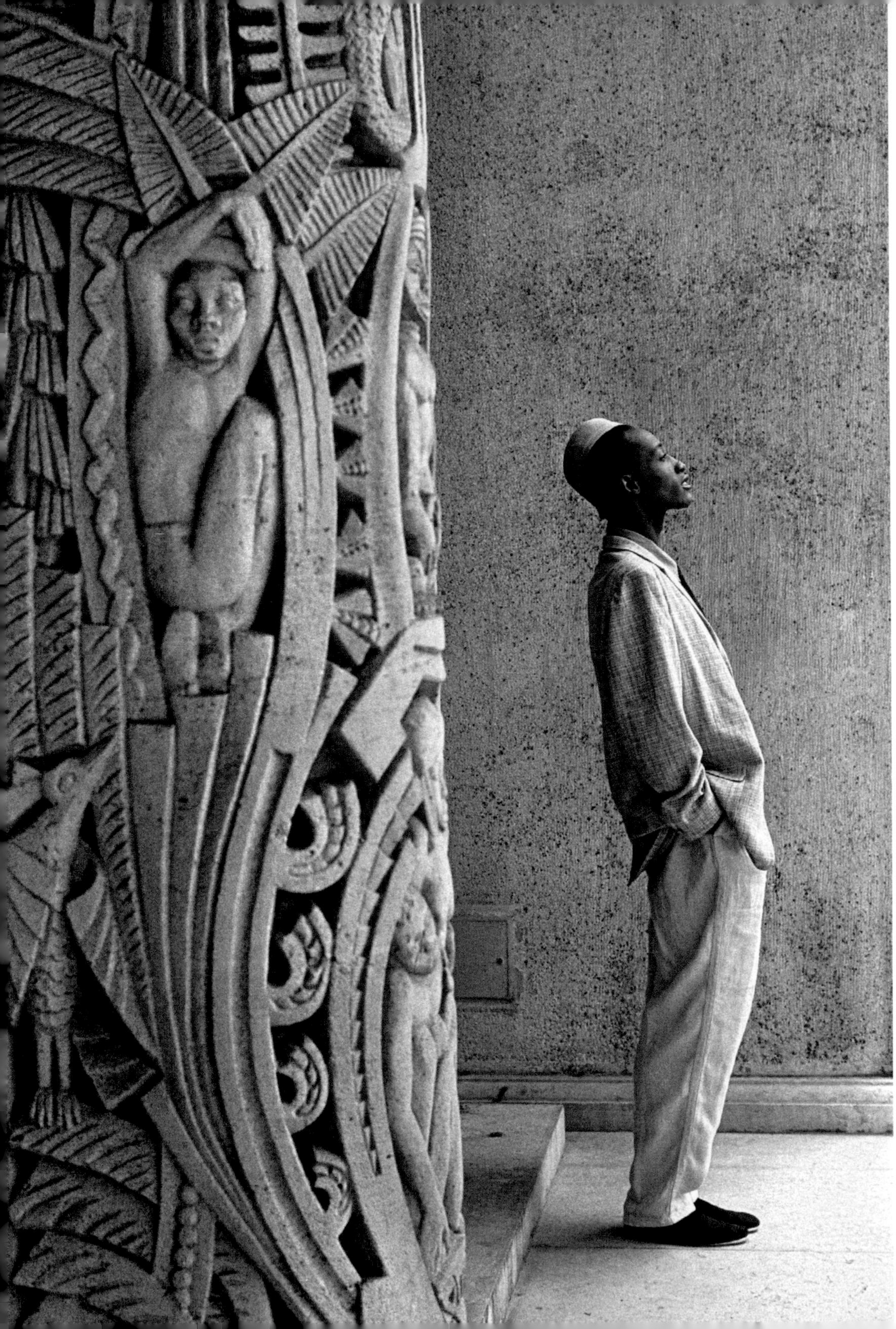

Turn, forever going to your other side,
turn your body on the space, even there,
on the trace, the work itself that it bestows, the infinite,
the invertible place that it brings everywhere,
the shock in this place or on the other side:
disappear into the face of the sun.

Face opposite Your Face, holding me upright
next to You, shaped, my body
as the unuttered letter, arched in desire,
back against the void. Behind me the world is raised:
songbirds, smoke rings, lush ferns, gangrenes,
haltings, inordinate embryos, all that makes,
unmakes language, builds it up, and, at the same
time, refutes it, offends it. Here lives meaning, and there
meaning does not exist, in what is named
and what cannot be named, in what
mixes, muddles, shows itself; in what
hides, obscures, illumines, disappears.

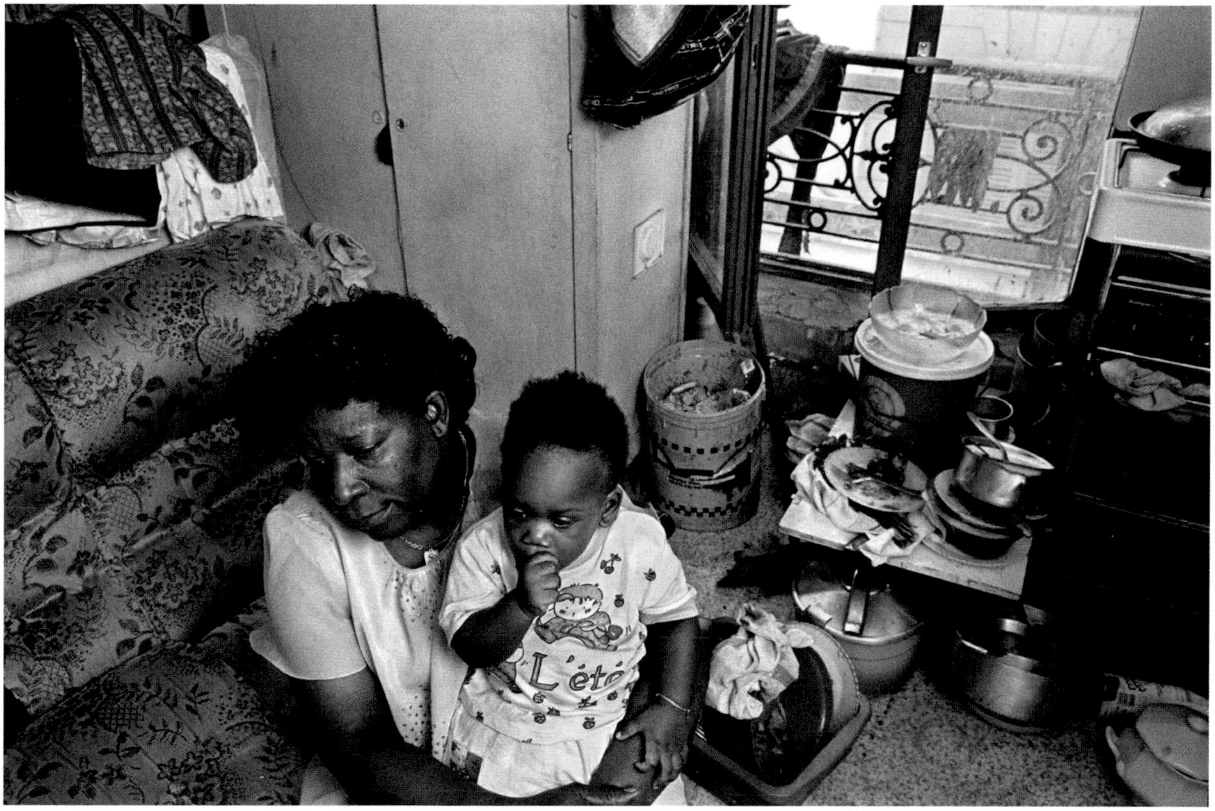
L'été

The eye riveted to the gap in the dark room:
the room is walled in by gazes,
oppressed. Gazes that know, surging back,
ruined, refused; gazes that don't
know, undamaged, pushed away.
Misplaced bundles thrown down pell-mell after
what senseless voyage, in the depths of
what defeat, for what end detached.
The unavoidable, ostentatious sofa bed, suffocating
with blooming presence in the middle of which
we sit down for the pose, taking care to stay
on the edge of white exile.

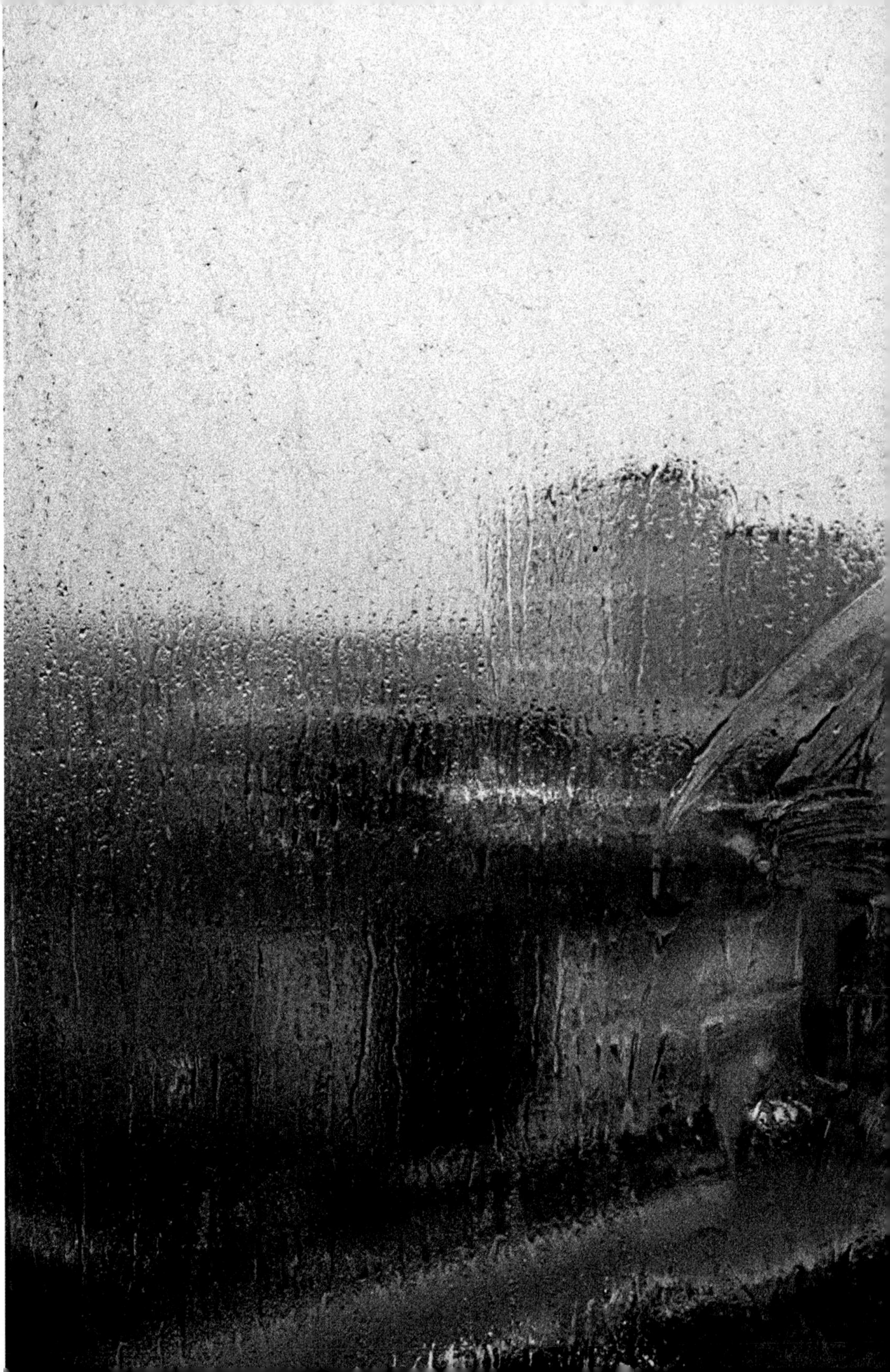

By which the distance between body
and Text is shown, a distance that is, truth be told,
infinite. There, in the feeling-of-life, acceptance
transfigures, starves, pain mixes
with joy, then, in ecstasy, abandons it for what's higher up,
for the solar, makes the ground shake.
Here, the Text subjugates, instructs, corrects, pulls
the gaze downward, softens the body, arches it,
ruins it.

Nothing, all, fasti, brief menstruations,
one, the devil, who stays, says again, permiso,
fasti, strength, virtue, respect, the tree,
the hurdle, cursed cobblestone grinds, equinox,
graft the transformation, Vel toto.

Sidelong glance, captured in the blink of an eye.
On one side, behind the statement of identity on
display, dependence on the new
idol, on the new bible, on the new text,
resignation to what is. On the other,
the distance that says, in body and gesture,
distinction as much as difference,
as soon as the clear pleasure of performance
is satisfied with a vindictive and
vehement mimicry.

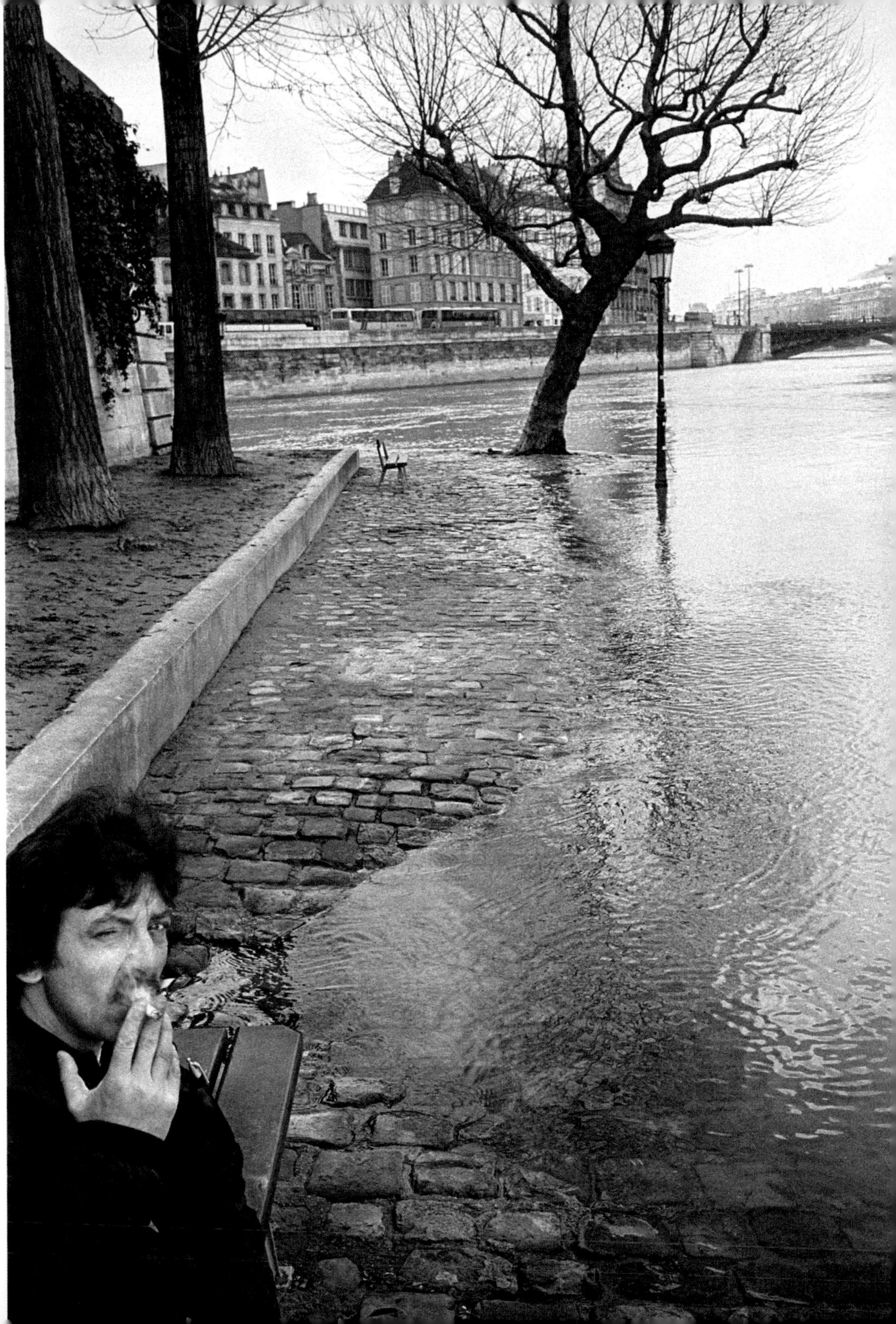

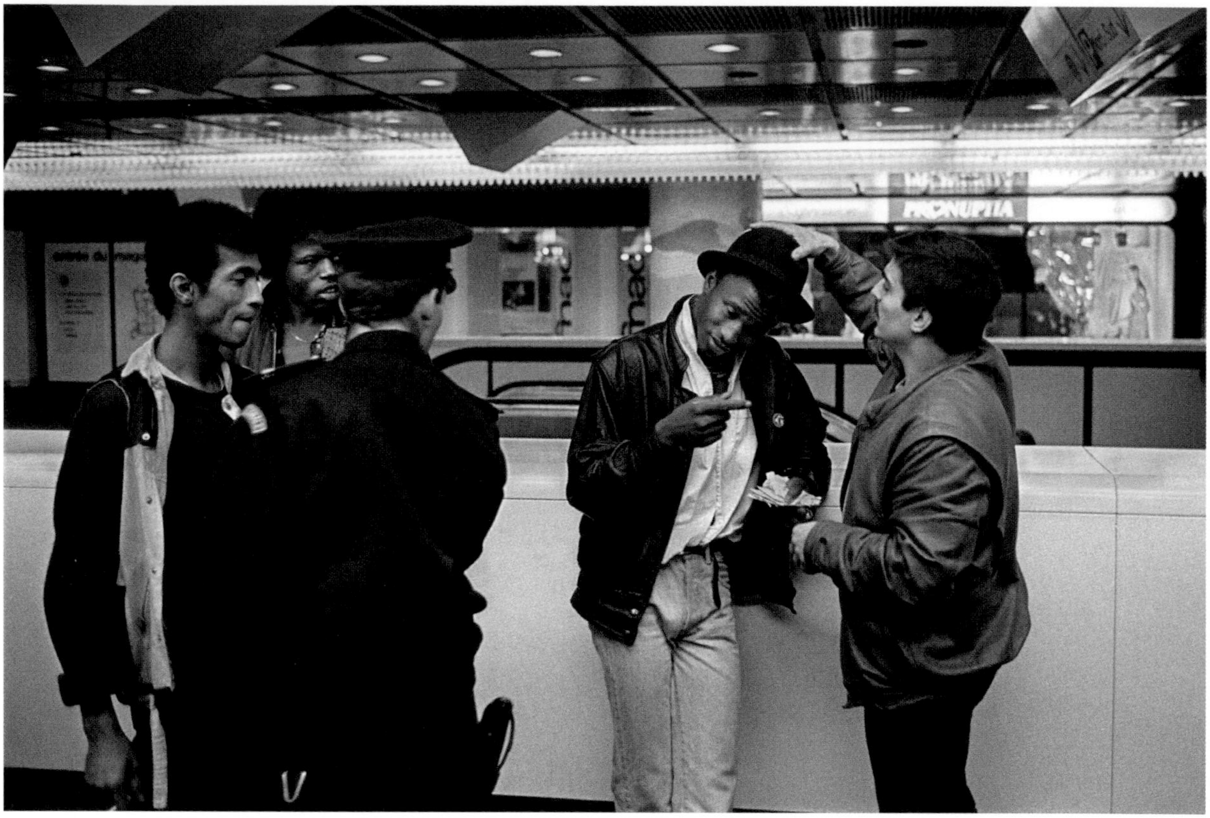
PRONUPTIA

To put a hand on the other, on his body,
grasp him, seize him, constrain him,
resembles the act of "placing a sign over,"
just as a certain language operates,
entirely oriented toward mastery and marking,
a language toward which the tag fittingly
thumbs its nose.

Each is equally hallucinatory,
one like the other, devoid of modesty.
The opposite of the approach, full of
consideration, which consists of going to
encounter the other, of signaling
toward the world, to call it and welcome it.

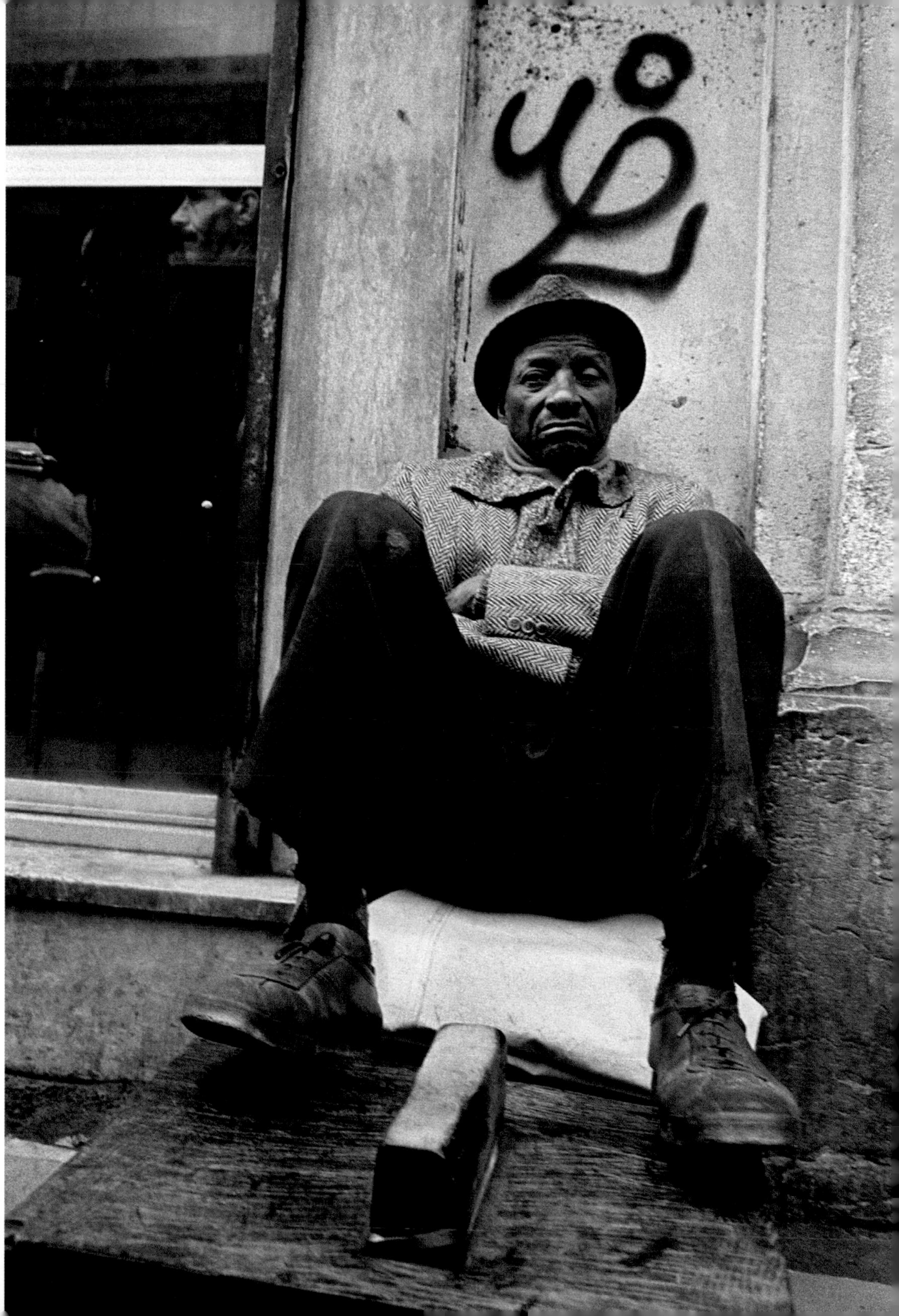

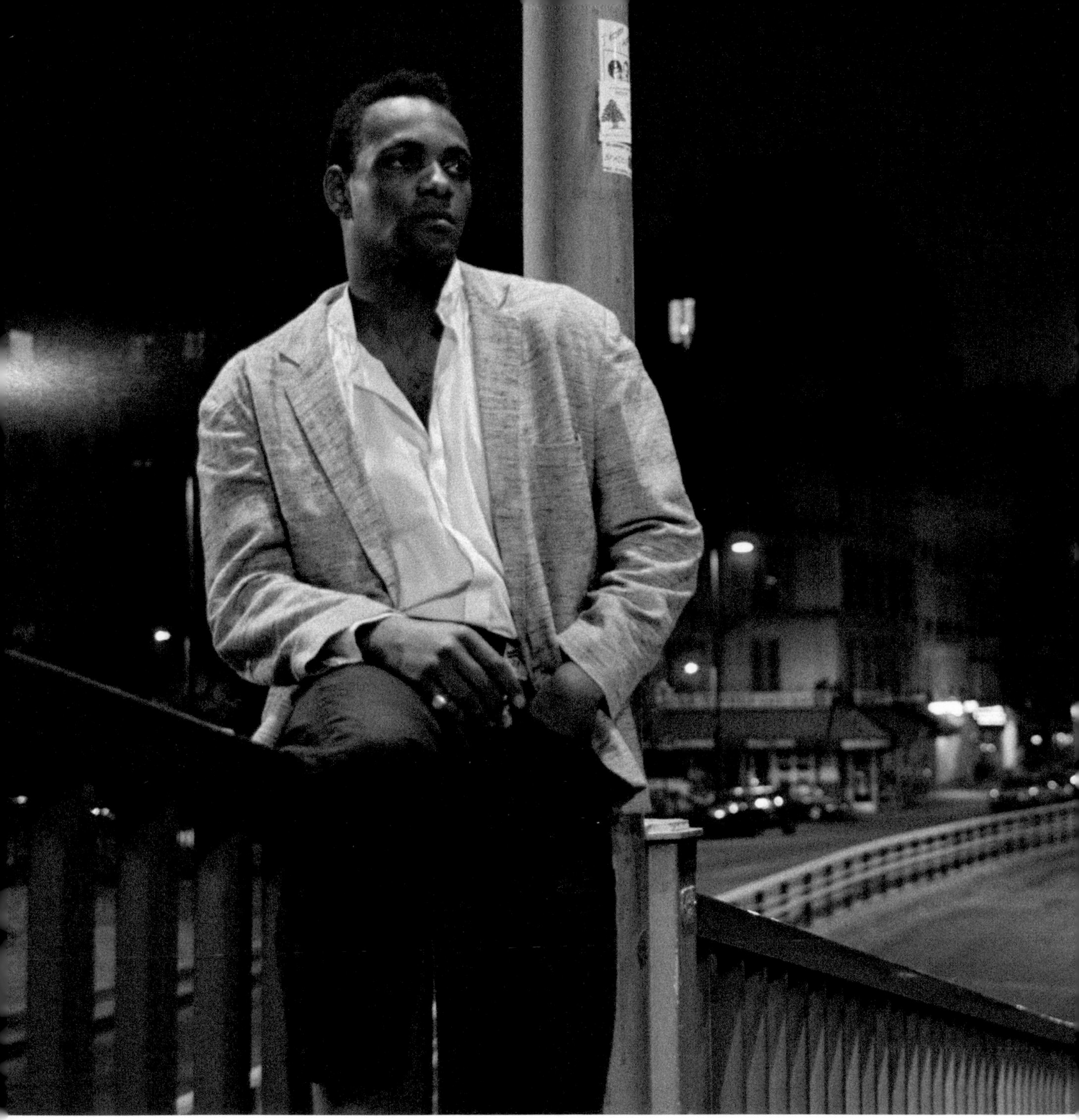

This Tang poem, from the night of time (three millennia), signs carved on tortoiseshell and buffalo bones:

Mind's mirror bright, reflection without obstruction,
silent translucence surrounds sand-grain realms.
Ten thousand images tangled between shadow and showing,
but a pearl of light, with no inside or out.

What the hand seizes thus, what speech cries, this verse that the word signifies, this one, is at the same time made visible and hopelessly obscured. A tree there, simple presence exposed, held, against the backing of sky; the hand, in grasping, imposes, disposes, elucidates, decides about presence, re-presents. The thing, henceforth, takes on meaning only in relationship to the hand. But the hand, in turn, can no longer define itself except in relationship to the thing. Eventually, the hand is so subjugated that its texture transforms to resemble the thing itself.

This bias of vanity, of ostentatious pride, of modesty, of unsettling elegance, (these long wise hands, one tightly holding an immense blade over the abatis), all this that acts, doesn't work sometimes without the intention of residing with virtue, in an unheard-of way.

In the end, which to fear the most? The scorching sun, with its great drought, that cuts your necks. The cane that minces your body, invisibly. Or the machine whose wake splits your heart? Whichever it is, here I am now, all stained without any of this having been settled.

That the vast sky would come here in its entirety onto the cutting edge of my saber. I keep immemorial protections about me, a place where I can preserve myself in the body's crossroads.

To turn your body onto something, just the same, in the in-between of a world where *to make*, with hand and speech, even fettered by irons, was identified with letting presence blossom and collecting it; and from another world where *to make* now signifies manufacturing. The pale crystals the factory discharges illustrate, furthermore, the state of man joined to machinery: crushed, steamed, pulverized, the body turns toward its own misery, worn out, ghost more than shadow, wandering in labyrinths with blind, abrupt walls, in the hoarse air lit only by a skylight, such a long moon.

The hand is a "thing apart." Joined, the two hands assemble all time's fragments; they gather subterranean memory and silence. They bring us back, turning to speech's other side, to presence's other side, to all places of clairvoyance and protection.

Unlike speech that spends its time running after itself, the hand that opens will never sink into bitterness. At the most, by force of grasping and fashioning, perhaps in some ways it will ruin itself, exhaust itself. The hand is always placed in the main-tenant, the now, the hand-holding, of time, but not the fleeting moment that sees future time vanish into the past: the main-tenance of time, in the interview and conversation between memory and the *to-come* that it welcomes. And so, this perpetual interview is, in an essential sense, a recollection.

From hand to hand, armed with the password, like this everything goes forth and arrives at its destination. Time turns its millstone, spatters the air: what has happened is nothing more than a rain of stars. The newly sharpened blade in both hands to splendidly begin again, leave everything in pieces.

Contributors

Victoria Baena is a research fellow in English and Modern Languages at Gonville & Caius College, University of Cambridge. She received her PhD in comparative literature from Yale in 2021, and her essays and reviews have appeared in *Boston Review*, *Dissent*, *Diacritics*, and elsewhere. She has taught courses on translation and on literature and revolution at Yale College, Bard Microcollege at Brooklyn Public Library, and the Yale Prison Education Initiative.

South African **Dineo Seshee Bopape** is a Polokwane-born multidisciplinary artist who combines a myriad of mediums using sounds, videos, and organic elements. Bopape's material and immaterial objects engulf the audience and attempt to understand the world and its narratives. Influenced by literature, thinkers, TV, books, music, popular culture, and recordings, Bopape creates experimental and playful video works and sculptural installations that reflect various aspects of culture. She finds inspiration in the metaphysical, spiritual, and cultural aspects of the earth—soil, clay, dust—which she reconstitutes as artistic forms that gently let the audience mediate and make their own interpretations.

David Damoison is a photographer of Martinican descent based in France.

Eric Fishman is an educator, writer, and translator. His most recent translation is *Outside: Poetry and Prose* by André du Bouchet (Bitter Oleander Press). He is currently translating a selected volume of poetry by Monchoachi. Eric is also a founding editor of *Young Radish*, a magazine of poetry and art by kids and teens.

Rodrigo Flores Sánchez (Mexico City, 1977) is a poet interested in experimentation, collaboration, and cross-disciplinary inquiry. He is the author of five poetry collections: *Ventana cerrada* (2020), *Tianguis* (2013), *Zalagarda* (2011), *estimado cliente* (2005 and 2007), and *baterías* (2006). He and Dolores Dorantes co-wrote *Intervenir/Intervene* (Ugly Duckling Presse, translated by Jen Hofer). His poems were collected in the two-author volume *Flores + Espina* alongside the work of Uruguayan poet Eduardo Espina.

Verónica Gerber Bicecci is a visual artist who writes. Her work has been exhibited internationally and she has published several books, including *Conjunto vacío*, which was awarded the 3rd International Aura Estrada Literature Prize. She also curated a selection of artworks from La Caixa Collection, exhibited in Whitechapel Gallery, London, in 2020. She presently teaches in Mexico City in the SOMA art program, a space dedicated to cultural and artistic exchange.

Scotia Gilroy is a literary translator from Vancouver, Canada, now based in Kraków, Poland. She studied English literature at Simon Fraser University and Polish language and literature at the Jagiellonian University's Centre for Polish Language and Culture. She was a mentee in the National Centre for Writing's Emerging Translator Mentorship in Norwich, England, in 2016/2017. Her translations have been published by *Panel Magazine*, *Widma*, *Asymptote*, *Tablet*, Brill, Terra Librorum, Comma Press, and Indiana University Press.

Christina MacSweeney's work has been recognized in a number of important awards: her translation of Valeria Luiselli's *The Story of My Teeth* was awarded the 2016 Valle Inclán Translation Prize and was shortlisted for the Dublin Literary Award (2017). Her most recent translations include fiction and nonfiction by Verónica Gerber Bicecci, Daniel Saldaña París, Elvira Navarro, Julián Herbert, Jazmina Barrera, and Karla Suárez. She has contributed to various anthologies of Latin American literature.

Monchoachi was born in 1946, in Martinique. His writing is marked by the astonishing character of the Creole language, a language rich in its very poverty, having preserved a speech unaltered by Western rationality, which is reflected in particular in its articulations and the constant play that inhabits it with the invisible. There he finds a resource from which to draw: what the word as such has to say about our relation to the world, a world obstructed and deafened by its present course. Following a period of bilingual publication, Monchoachi transported Creole into the body of a writing that presents itself with a French surface, and there makes its own mark.

Robin Myers is a Mexico City-based translator and poet. Recent book-length translations include *Copy* by Dolores Dorantes (Wave Books), *The Dream of Every Cell* by Maricela Guerrero (Cardboard House Press), *Tonight: The Great Earthquake* by Leonardo Teja (PANK Books), *The Book of Explanations* by Tedi López Mills (Deep Vellum Publishing), *The Science of Departures* by Adalber Salas Hernández (Kenning Editions), and *Another Life* by Daniel Lipara (Eulalia Books).

Marie NDiaye was born in 1967 in Pithiviers, France. She is the author of around twenty novels, plays, collections of stories, and nonfiction books, which have been translated into numerous languages. She's received the Prix Femina and the Prix Goncourt, France's highest literary honor, and her plays are in the repertoire of the Comédie-Française.

Monika Sznajderman has been the head of Czarne, Poland's leading publisher of literary nonfiction, since 1996. She is a cultural anthropologist, author, and editor of numerous works of cultural criticism. Her father, Marek Sznajderman (whose story, among others, is told in *The Pepper Forgers*), was a renowned cardiologist, and her grandfather (also in the book) was a renowned neurologist. Her husband is Andrzej Stasiuk, one of Poland's best-known writers of fiction and literary journalism.

Emily Yae Won is a literary and art translator working in Korean and in English. Recent translations include Samuel Beckett's *Murphy*, Jennifer Croft's *Homesick*, Han Junghyun's *Kyoko and Kyoji*, Hwang Jungeun's *DD's Umbrella* (forthcoming from Tilted Axis Press, 2023), Deborah Levy's *The Cost of Living*, Valeria Luiselli's *Tell Me How It Ends*, Maggie Nelson's *The Argonauts*, Chris Ware's *Rusty Brown*, and stories by Han Kang, Pak Kyongni, and Yi SangWoo.

Yi SangWoo (b. 1988) made his debut when he was awarded the 2011 Munhakdongne New Writer in Fiction Prize. His stories have been collected in 프리즘 [Prism] (Munhakdongne, 2015) and *warp* (Workroom Press, 2017). His most recent book, 두 사람이 걸어가 [Two people walk by] (Moonji, 2020), collects interlinked stories together into a long form and reflects his ongoing interest in exploring the visual, aural, and formal facets of the story and the book.

Credits

Rodrigo Flores Sánchez, *Ventana cerrada*. Mexico City: LibrosUNAM, 2020.

Verónica Gerber Bicecci, *Las palabras y las imágenes*. Mexico City: Minerva Editorial, 2019. The text is a re-writing of "Les mots et les images" by René Magritte, from *La Révolution surréaliste*, 1929.

Monchoachi (text) and David Damoison (photos), *Paris Caraïbe: Le voyage des sens*. Bayonne: Atlantica, 2002. Later sections of "Le beau rêve qu'on déplie et qu'on tend…" from *Éloge de la servilité*. Vauclin: Lakouzémi, 2007.

Marie NDiaye, *Un pas de chat sauvage*. Paris: Flammarion/Musées d'Orsay et de l'Orangerie, 2019.

Monika Sznajderman, *Fałszerze pieprzu: Historia rodzinna*. Wołowiec: Czarne, 2016.

Yi SangWoo, "배와 버스가 지나가고" from Busan Biennale 2020
Words at an Exhibition: 열 장의 이야기와 다섯 편의 시 [*an exhibition in ten chapters and five poems*] (Artistic Director Jacob Fabricius). Seoul: Busan Biennale Organizing Committee & Mediabus, 2020.

CALICO

The Calico Series, published biannually by
Two Lines Press, captures vanguard works
of translated literature in stylish, collectible
editions. Each Calico is a vibrant snapshot
that explores one aspect of our present
moment, offering the voices of previously
inaccessible, highly innovative writers from
around the world today.